The Ba

"And stay away from your so-called mates. They're not the ones who ended up here . . . and they're not the ones who will go to the Detention Centre next time."

"Feeling nervous?" said Mr Sampson.

"No," said Lol. He was certainly excited at the thought of working with cars and relieved that the magistrate had decided to send him here and not to the detention centre.

Over the entrance was a large official looking sign — The Sumner House Project. Underneath, hand painted on an old piece of wood was another one — Bessie's Banger Boys.

Lol was surprised to find how much he enjoyed working on the old banger Bessie, and the companionship of the others.

He was to discover just how much their friendship meant when he found himself once more unwittingly involved with his "so-called mates" and a stolen car.

The Banger Boys is Anne Fussell's first novel. An exciting read for all readers of 10+.

THE BANGER BOYS

Anne Fussell

Hippo Books
Scholastic Publications Limited
London

Scholastic Publications Ltd.,
10 Earlham Street, London WC2H 9LN, UK

Scholastic Inc.,
730 Broadway, New York, NY 10003, USA

Scholastic Tab Publications Ltd.,
123 Newkirk Road, Richmond Hill,
Ontario, L4C 3G5, Canada

Ashton Scholastic Pty. Ltd.,
P O Box 579, Gosford, New South Wales,
Australia

Ashton Scholastic Ltd.,
165 Marua Road, Panmure, Auckland 6,
New Zealand

First published by Scholastic Publications Ltd., 1986

Cover illustration by Barry Wilkinson

ISBN 0 590 70536 9

Made and printed by Cox and Wyman Ltd
Reading, Berks

Phototypeset by AKM Associates (UK) Ltd
Ajmal House, Hayes Road, Southall, London

Chapter One

It was dark in the corridor and the tobacco-brown paint that seemed to cover every surface made it worse. Lol sat staring at his feet. He had been seated in the same position for more than fifteen minutes, ever since he and his parents had arrived. They all sat in a line on the hard wooden bench but no one talked. In a way, that made it worse. The silence. He felt he would have preferred it if they had told him off, shouted at him, anything.

At last the courtroom door opened and his name was called out. Even after all that waiting it still came as a shock and he leapt to his feet as if stung.

As they walked in he could see Mr Gilroy, the solicitor, already seated at a small table. He smiled fleetingly and beckoned Lol to his side. His parents self-consciously filed onto the bench behind them.

Lol glanced quickly to his right. A uniformed police inspector sat behind a similar table, his cap placed neatly in front of him alongside a pile of papers and two or three bulging folders.

"All rise."

The usher's deep sonorous voice resounded through the courtroom, filling every corner. Mr Gilroy stood up, so did the police inspector and, from the shuffling Lol could hear behind him, so did everyone else.

There was a click, a door opened, and in silence three magistrates walked in, settling themselves behind the high wooden bench facing Lol and the rest of the court. The one in the middle, the chairwoman, wore a hat that looked like one of his father's hydrangeas, with hundreds of tiny blue petals that bounced gently with every movement of her head. On either side of her sat a man, middle-aged, grey-haired, indistinguishable.

Everyone in the courtroom then sat again except Lol, who automatically remained standing, and he realized that he was actually getting used to court procedure; when to stand, when to sit, when to speak up and when to make do with a polite "Yes, ma'am."

It did not take long. Lol admitted each of the four charges of taking and driving away vehicles without permission. He sat, and the Inspector then gave details of each of the offences and of his previous court appearances.

Then Mr Gilroy got up to speak and, for the first time, Lol hung his head, but more with embarrassment than shame. To hear someone trying to tell the court what a good son you are, always helping at home, kind to old ladies and sick animals, a victim of the media's onslaught making young people want things they can't have, was agonising. Finally Mr Gilroy handed the magistrates written school and probation reports, then took his seat again beside Lol.

If they signalled to each other Lol did not see it but suddenly, as one, the three magistrates picked up their papers and left the courtroom, marching one behind the other through the small side door. They were going to decide what to do with him. Lol knew the form. He had seen it all before.

He did consider turning round to talk to his parents, but what could he say? Instead he stared at his feet, itching for it all to be over whatever his fate.

Twenty minutes ticked away in almost total silence. Apart from the police inspector who chatted for a few moments to Mr Gilroy and the usher, sharing a joke with the young social worker who popped her head round the door looking for someone, there was silence.

"All rise."

Everyone leapt to their feet again and, as before, Lol was left standing on his own.

The woman in the hydrangea hat cleared her throat, straightened her papers and, fixing Lol with a steely stare, began speaking.

"Well, Laurence, you have admitted taking the cars without permission and that of course is to your credit, but it does not make it any the less wrong for you to have done it at all.

"Young people today have too lax an attitude towards other people's property. You see something, you want it, so you just take it, never considering that some person has probably worked long and hard to buy it. You want it immediately — for nothing.

"Unfortunately this is not the first, nor the second time you have appeared before a court because you consider you have a right to take anything that takes your fancy, and we consider it perfectly proper that you should go to a detention centre . . ."

Lol's chest tightened and for a moment he couldn't breathe properly. Detention Centre. His probation officer had warned him they might consider it but when the words were actually spoken by the magistrate he realized he hadn't really prepared himself for the possibility at all.

"But . . ." the woman continued, bringing Lol back to reality. "We have allowed ourselves to be persuaded by what your probation officer, Mr Sampson, says and give you one more chance.

"We are not absolutely certain that we are doing the right thing but we have been persuaded to take a gamble on you. Remember this. If you get in any further trouble at all there will be no second chances. You will be shut away. Do you understand?"

Lol nodded, then hurriedly added a weak, "Yes, ma'am."

"Right, providing that is clearly understood, we propose to make an order that you attend the Sumner House Project for a total of 240 hours, starting this week. Do you agree?"

Again Lol nodded.

"And you will pay £120 costs and damages."

With that, the three magistrates stood up, gave a formal half-bow to the court and left again. The clerk turned to Lol.

"Your probation officer will explain everything to you. Written notification of the order will be sent to you within the next seven days."

Lol found he was trembling and his throat raspingly dry. Behind him, his mother was nudging his father, pointing something out, but his father remained ramrod straight, face palely impassive. Finally Mr Sampson came over, clutching his bulging briefcase to his chest, and they followed him through the door marked Probation Service Only.

"Excuse me for being obtuse Mr Sampson," his mother said as soon as they were all seated, "but I don't think I quite understand. Does this mean they can still send him away if they want to?"

Mr Sampson leaned back in his chair, placing his finger-tips together, and bouncing them slightly against each other.

"Basically, Mr and Mrs Lord, what the magistrates have said is that Laurence can attend the Project as I recommended for a total of 240 hours, which will be spread over the next six months. If during that time he behaves, then nothing more will happen. If, however, he commits another offence he will be brought back to the court and will almost certainly be sent to a detention centre. The magistrates made that very clear."

"I'm still not sure I approve," Lol's father said. "I've heard about the Sumner House Project. If cars get him into trouble it seems pure folly to me to send him somewhere to play with cars. It will be more of a lark than a punishment."

"I admit that at first glance it might seem like that," Mr Sampson agreed. "But there is more to the scheme than that. The idea is that by allowing the youngsters to work with vehicles — the very things that fascinate them so much — they will develop a more responsible attitude towards them."

"Surely if he drives a car it will be illegal? After all, he's not even fifteen yet."

"Any driving — and believe me, there isn't a great deal of that — is done on private property so there is absolutely no question of breaking the law. And most of the boys' time will be spent working on the cars, not driving them."

When he realized they had no more questions, Mr Sampson asked if he could talk to Lol alone.

"Right, Laurence," he said, walking round to sit perched on the edge of the table. "Cards on the table. This is absolutely your last chance. It took every ounce of my persuasive powers to prevent them sending you away. Next time — if there ever is a next time — I don't think anyone could save you.

"If you take advantage of what is being put in front of you, you will find it rewarding work, and fun. A word of advice . . ." Lol drew in his breath sharply. "Here we go", he thought. ". . . stay away from your so-called mates. They are not the ones who ended up here today, and they're not the ones who will go to a detention centre next time."

Lol leaned back, sticking his legs out in front of him.

"O.K.," he said grudgingly. "I'll go. But only because I have to, don't expect me to enjoy it."

"Go with an attitude like that and you

might as well book your place at the detention centre right now. Still, it's your funeral. I've done everything I can, now it's all up to you."

Outside in the corridor his parents were waiting, his mother looking distinctly ill at ease, and together the four of them went along the dark dreary hall and out into the street.

"I'll take you along there tomorrow, to introduce you to everyone," Mr Sampson told Lol. "After that you can make your own way there. I'll pick you up at 9.30, O.K?"

Lol nodded. "O.K."

"Goodbye, Mr and Mrs Lord." Mr Sampson turned and walked back into the court building.

Lol and his parents crossed the road to the car park. The little Mini, his father's pride and joy, was sparkling clean, not a scrap of rust or smear of dirt anywhere. Although Lol usually fought to have the front seat, this time as soon as the passenger door was open, he got in the back. Out of the way, he hoped.

At first nobody said anything, though Lol could see his father's hands tightening on the steering wheel until the knuckles went white.

"Well, I hope you're pleased with yourself." The tirade began when they stopped at a set of lights. His father glared back at Lol "Can you imagine how your mother feels? All her friends know about you, you know. But do you care? Not a bit. You never think of anyone else, do you? Well, this is the last time. Any more trouble and we wash our hands of you, detention centre or not. We can't go on like this." He was interrupted by a toot from the car behind as the lights turned to green.

"All right, all right," he told the anonymous driver. "What's your hurry?"

It always fascinated Lol that his father actually drove within the 30 mph limit. He didn't know anyone else who did, even the police. Sometimes he found himself longing to see the little red arrow on the speedometer creep past 30 mph — but it never did.

It wasn't just speed that made cars so fascinating to Lol. It was something about the feeling of power driving gave you. To put your foot down on the accelerator and feel the car surge forward, to brake and feel it fighting against you. It was like no other feeling.

When he had a car he wouldn't drive like his father, slowly and cautiously. He would roar into corners and laugh when the car tried to break from his control. He could handle any car.

As soon as they got inside the house Lol went straight to his room and shut the door. Quickly he took off the suit his mother had insisted he wore to court. Carelessly he threw it onto the chair, changed into jeans and sweat shirt and slipped his feet into running shoes.

He put on his Walkman and pressed the start button. The heavy thumping beat of Status Quo hammered his head and he rocked backwards and forwards in time to the music. He needed to get out.

Pushing the ear-phones from his ears he pulled on his favourite cycling cap, then he ran down the stairs two at a time, pausing long enough to snatch up his jacket from the hall cupboard.

"Where are you off to?" His father's voice came from the sitting room but Lol hurried on, pretending he hadn't heard.

"I said, where are you going?" His father appeared behind him in the kitchen. Lol turned.

"Sorry, Dad. I didn't hear you," he lied. "I just thought I'd go for a ride on my bike." They stared at each other, hostile eyes locked together.

"Mind you clean it up when you get back. You know you left it out all last night. If it had rained it would be rusty by now."

Lol sighed. "O.K. Dad." He opened the kitchen door quickly before his father could think of anything else to nag him about. His bike was where he had left it, leaning against the shed.

Lol always felt good when he looked at it. It really was a beauty. Grey and sleek with ten gears that could send it bowling along faster than . . . well, faster than his father usually drove his car!

Pulling the ear-phones back down over

his ears he swung into the saddle and let the bike roll down the drive. A quick glance right and left, and he began pedalling down the road. In his ears the sounds of Status Quo boomed out, and he pedalled faster and faster, feeling the wind rushing against his face.

The frantic blasting of a horn broke through the sounds and brought him back to reality with a bang.

"Are you crazy or something?"

Lol looked round to see a man's angry face staring at him through the open window of his car.

"You crazy fool, you nearly went right under my wheels. Take those stupid things off your ears."

"Ah, belt up!" Lol flashed a V-sign at the man but as he cycled away his heart was thumping from a mixture of fear and excitement. The road took him down by the amusement arcade, but when he saw the bright flashing lights outside it he pulled in to the pavement and stopped. Baz and Greg would be there, they always were, and he didn't fancy meeting them now. He'd just about had his fill of bother for a while.

He neatly turned the bike in a wide loop and, pedalling hard, made his way home.

His mother was alone when he went into the house to find a rag to clean off the bike's wheels.

"Fancy a nice cup of tea, love? That'll warm you up," she asked him, and he nodded. He didn't really want one but he felt he couldn't refuse.

When he came in after putting his bike away in the shed he found a plate of scones on the table too. He sat down and idly began picking the sultanas out, placing them in a small pile on his plate to be enjoyed together afterwards.

"Laurence!" His mother slapped his hand.

"It tastes better this way," he protested.

"Laurence." She sat down in the chair beside him. He looked up with an uncomfortable feeling inside. He hoped this wasn't going to be a heart-to-heart, they always left him feeling acutely embarrassed.

"Yes, Mum."

"You will at least try to make a go of this, won't you, love? It's so important to your father. I don't think he could stand it if you were sent away to that detention centre."

Lol, who had been stirring his teacup with enough determination to dissolve two bowlsful of sugar rather than the one spoonful he had put in, looked at his mother.

"Yes, Mum, I'll make a go of it, honest."

He was already awake when his mother knocked on his bedroom door the next morning. He called out "Come in," and when she entered he saw she was carrying a cup of tea. Wonders would never cease.

"Thanks, Mum." He stretched out a hand to take it from her. "A last drink for the condemned man?"

"Very funny! Now hurry up and get dressed. I've started your breakfast."

When he did emerge downstairs fifteen minutes later she looked at him disapprovingly.

"You can't go out looking like that," she told him.

He glanced down at his clothes. Sneakers, jeans and an old black pullover.

"What's wrong with them?"

"You look so scruffy. Look, I've ironed you a nice clean shirt and your black trousers would be so much nicer.

"Mum," his voice was rough. "It isn't a flippin' fashion show I'm going to. It'll be really filthy there. I can hardly go looking like a Burton window dummy."

"There's no need to snap like that, just because I care whether you look like a ragbag or not."

He sighed. If he wasn't quick he'd be getting the "I can feel a migraine coming on" line. "Honest, Mum, it doesn't matter what I wear, does it?" She left the eggs and bacon spitting in the pan on the cooker and gave him a soft touch to his cheek.

"Sit down and eat your breakfast."

He was still seated when his father came in from walking the dog.

"Hello, Rocket, had a good time?" Lol leaned down to pat the dog and began to cut up some of his toast.

"Don't feed the dog at the table. How many times do I have to tell you?" His father's voice was curt.

"One bit of bacon isn't going to hurt," Lol protested.

"He'll get fat. He doesn't get enough exercise as it is."

Lol kept silent. That was his fault. He was supposed to take Rocket for regular walks but somehow there was always something else to do. He would not win that argument.

"What time does Mr Sampson come?" his mother asked as she joined them at the table. Lol knew that she knew perfectly well. She had checked and double-checked it the previous day.

"Nine-thirty." There was no point making an issue of it.

"And what time do you think you'll be back?" He sighed, he had already told her several times that he didn't know.

"Mum, I don't know."

"There's no need to take that tone with your mother," his father spoke from behind his newspaper. "She was only asking."

"But I've told her I don't know, and I *don't* know." He clattered his knife down on the plate and with a loud scraping sound pushed his chair away from the table. He stormed out of the kitchen. For once, he got clear before his father could call him back.

He stood in his room, his face red with anger, his breath coming in short little gulps. He felt like he'd lived that scene dozens of times before. Exactly the same. Nothing changed.

He looked at the bed, thinking for a second that he might make it, but then decided not to. Why bother? Everything was so boring.

There was a loud buzz at the front door. Lol glanced at his watch — nine-thirty. He didn't move, just listened. He heard footsteps in the hall, then the door opening, then voices, his father's and Mr Sampson's. Then the expected yell.

"Laurence." He didn't answer.

"Laurence!" The voice was louder now, so loud even he couldn't pretend he hadn't heard it.

"Yes," he bellowed down, not bothering to open the bedroom door.

"It's Mr Sampson." He waited several more seconds.

"O.K., I'm coming." Then, quite deliberately, he waited almost five minutes before opening the door and going down the stairs.

Mr Sampson was sitting in the lounge looking as comfortable as if he were an everyday visitor. Lol's father and mother were hovering nearby and he could hear them chatting about the weather. The weather! thought Lol. When he went in Mr Sampson immediately got up.

"Ah there you are, we'd better be off.

Don't want to be late on your first day, do we?"

Lol took his anorak off the peg.

"Oh Laurence, not that one," his mother said, going and fetching his new blue one from the cupboard. "That's filthy."

Before Lol could protest, Mr Sampson interrupted.

"I think that one's fine, Mrs Lord," he said, indicating the one Lol held. "He'll probably get pretty filthy at the Project, I'm afraid."

Lol did not feel particularly grateful for this unwitting support and he noted that whereas his mother had taken little notice of his protests, Mr Sampson's were immediately heeded. The new anorak went back in the cupboard.

Mr Sampson led the way out. Lol's mother gave him a quick kiss on the cheek before he followed Mr Sampson down the path to his car.

"Nervous?" Mr Sampson glanced at Lol after they had been driving for several minutes in silence.

"No." It was the truth really. He was not nervous. A little curious and excited at the prospect of working with cars, but not nervous.

There was no more conversation until they turned off the main road into a small pot-holed lane and, after a few hundred metres, turned into a gateway which led to two rather battered garages, end to end, and, some distance away and partially hidden by trees a tall, gloomy Victorian house.

Over the entrance was a large official-looking sign — The Sumner House Project. Underneath, hand-painted on an old piece of wood was another one — Bessie's Banger Boys.

Mr Sampson parked his car outside the house and led Lol round the side and into the garages. Inside it was bedlam. The air was filled with the sound of banging and music coming from a portable radio balanced on top of some lopsided shelves.

Three pairs of feet stuck out from under a red Cortina that was raised up on some ramps. After several moments one of the pairs of legs began to inch its way out from under the car, followed by the others. Finally a large bearded man emerged. He was covered with dirt and grease, but still shook hands with Lol and Mr Sampson.

The other pairs of legs belonged to two boys about the same age as Lol. They stood, leaning against the work bench, watching.

"This is Laurence Lord," said Mr Sampson, and Mr Jackson gave him a wide smile.

"Hello, Laurence. Right, I'll just go and get some papers from the house." He turned to the two boys.

"These two are Alan and Benjamin — Biffo to his friends — they'll show you around. I'll be back in a few minutes."

After the two men had gone the three boys stood looking at each other. Finally the tall black boy, who was wearing a striped tea-cosy hat, shrugged, stepped forward and spoke.

"O.K., well, this is garage one. Most of the work is done here. Jacko shows us how to do things and then he lets us have a go ourselves. He's O.K. really, so long as you obey the rules and don't muck about. Hey man, is your name really Laurence, that's real posh?" He grinned.

"Everyone calls me Lol."

"Yeah well, I suppose that's a bit better," Biffo said.

Lol wandered around the garage looking at the bits and pieces stacked neatly around the sides and on the bench. Then he stopped beside the big red car, lovingly stroking the long sleek bonnet with his hands.

"Is this what we work on?" he asked the boys.

"That's a good one," said the other boy scathingly. "No, this is Jacko's own car. He lets us look but not touch, that way he guarantees it keeps running," and he exploded into peals of laughter at his own joke.

"No man," Biffo interrupted. "We work with Bessie, she's one hell of a lady."

Lol was confused. He looked around the garage again but could see no sign of a woman.

"I didn't know girls could come here."

Again there were roars of laughter and both boys rocked from side to side.

"That's good, that's really good," the tall boy said, slapping his sides like some second-rate stand-up comic. "No women here!"

Lol felt the colour rising to his cheeks. He was embarrassed at having made what was obviously a stupid mistake and he turned on the two boys angrily.

"Well, who the hell is this stupid old Bessie then?" he shouted at them, hands on hips.

The two boys looked at each other, then, still grinning, led him through a small side door into the other garage.

"Man, that's Bessie, and ain't she something?" said Biffo pointing with an extravagant flourish into the garage.

Lol followed the line of his arm, and there in front of him he saw a huge crumpled wreck. There was no other way of describing the car, if a car was what it had once been.

There were no wheels, no bonnet, no windows. The headlamps hung out like dismembered eyes, the bumpers were buckled and twisted. Inside, the seats were ripped and filthy and the dashboard hung half off. Only the steering wheel seemed to be in working order.

"That's a car?" Lol couldn't keep the sarcasm out of his voice.

"Bessie ain't just a car," Biffo said, his face for once serious. "Bessie's a banger."

Chapter Two

Gradually, in ones and twos, the other boys came in until there were nine of them in all. Lol felt alone and out of it. They all seemed to know each other, and were laughing and joking as they lounged around the sides of the garage.

When Mr Jackson re-entered the sound slowly died away but the atmosphere was still light and easy.

"O.K. you lot," he crossed to stand by Lol. "We have a newcomer in our midst, Laurence Lord, another budding Lauda who wants to try and knock his teeth out smashing into other vehicles and have his mum come round to beat me up afterwards."

A laugh went round the garage, but Lol, the centre of unwanted attention, scowled.

"As most of you already know — but it

won't do you any harm hearing it again — the rules are very simple. I'm the boss. What I say goes — right?" and there was a little ragged chorus of "right".

"After that you learn as you go along. Now for today, Laurence . . ."

"Lol," Lol interrupted.

"O.K., Lol, you can work with Biffo." Lol did not miss the raised eyebrows Biffo shot at the boy next to him. "He'll show you the ropes and introduce you to the rest of the gang. O.K. everybody — work."

With that, the boys began to gather together metal boxes, rags, bottles of liquid and armfuls of tools.

"Right now man," Biffo said, rubbing his hands together, "seeing as how you and I are going to be teamed up, we'd better get started. How much do you know about cars?"

"There's nothing I can't drive, manual or automatic. And I don't need a key," Lol told him proudly.

"Not nicking them, stupid," Biffo scoffed. "Tuning 'em. Bessie ain't got no wheels on so she ain't going nowhere at all."

Lol felt his blood rising. He'd had just about enough of that guy's smart mouth. He took a menacing half step towards him.

"Hey man, no harm meant," said Biffo holding his hands up in front of him and grinning widely. "I was only joking. You sure are prickly. Look, a word of advice, meant friendly like, from an old, old hand. No one here wants to make you look a fool, generally everyone manages to do that on their own. You play the game and they play the game and everyone gets on all right. No point in fighting amongst ourselves is there — unless of course you don't like black boys with woolly hats?"

Lol laughed, he couldn't help it, and within a few minutes he was watching intently as Biffo showed him where the tools were kept. They worked silently together, and before they knew what time it was they became aware that the others had stopped work and were sitting on whatever they could find, eating their lunch.

With a look of relief, Biffo broke away from what he was doing and walked over to the bench, picking up a large brown paper bag. Then he squatted down on the floor so he could lean against several tyres that were piled up.

"You got anything to eat?" he asked Lol as he looked inside his paper bag.

"No — I didn't think. It doesn't matter though. I'm not really hungry."

"Don't be stupid. Have one of mine," and he handed the bag over.

"Thanks." Lol took a large, roughly-cut sandwich. "What is it?"

"Peanut butter and banana," Biffo told him, sinking his teeth into his own sandwich. There was silence as the boys munched.

"Where's Jacko?" Lol asked, suddenly noticing that he was not with them.

"He lives in that house," Biffo jerked his thumb over his shoulder. "His wife always makes him a nice hot meal, compensation sort of for having to mix with riff-raff like us."

"Is that what she thinks?" Lol's sandwich halted mid-way to his mouth.

" 'Course not, dope. She's great. A real laugh." They munched on.

"Want one?" The boy who had been standing by Biffo when Lol had first entered the garage now offered Lol his paper bag. "It's sardine."

Inwardly, Lol's stomach groaned. In fact, peanut butter and sardines rated pretty high on his list of non-favourite food but he didn't want to refuse. He felt his link with this group was still too tenuous.

"That's Alan," Biffo told Lol as he began to eat and Lol nodded hello. Biffo continued the introductions though they were punctuated by his taking frequent bites from his sandwich.

There was Zak, a tall and lanky coloured boy; Joseph, a blond-haired boy about Lol's size but big and beefy; Zippo, a big red-head; John, another black boy, who turned out to be the mechanical genius of the team; Des, who didn't look more than twelve but who, Biffo assured

Lol, was an ace driver; Tom, silent and sullen-looking, who Lol rarely heard speak, and finally Luke, whose main claim to fame was that he actually owned his own moped.

Each nodded at Lol as his name was mentioned, then went back to eating in silence.

"What are you here for?" Lol asked as he shared half of Biffo's cake.

"Same as everyone else, nicking cars," Biffo told him.

"What did you take?"

For a second Lol thought he had gone too far. Biffo's face remained impassive but he turned quickly to look Lol in the eye.

"Go on, Biffo, tell him what you did." The blond-haired boy (what was it Biffo had called him, Joseph?) gleefully egged him on. Lol was intrigued.

"Well I thought I'd like a bit of class," Biffo got to his feet, standing in front of the group like an actor on a stage. "And what's the classiest car you can get?"

"A Rolls Royce," they all chorused.

"Absolutely right, my friends, a Rolls Royce. So I thought I'd get me a Rolls Royce, and where do you find lots and lots of Rolls Royce?"

"Outside the Ritz," the chorus came back again.

Lol looked at Biffo in amazement but before the story could be completed, Jacko came back into the garage.

"O.K., lunch break over, back to work everyone. Zak, I want those oil drums taken outside, they make the place stink — and John, you left that tin of washers with the lid off, some are rusty. Give 'em a soaking in cleaning fluid."

They were all engrossed in their work for some time before Lol remembered the story Biffo had been telling.

"Did you really take a Roller?" he asked, his voice just a whisper.

"Sure. Piece of cake."

"Wow. I've never got anything better than a Cortina." Lol sounded crestfallen.

"They're so dim," Biffo turned on Lol, contempt in his voice. "They even leave the keys in them. Them fat cats don't give a damn."

"Didn't anyone see you?"

"No, all the doormen were too busy scraping and bowing — until it was too late."

"What are they like to drive?"

"Bee-ooo-tiful," Biffo rolled his eyes appreciatively. "Like riding along on a jet-propelled settee."

"How'd you get caught?"

"I didn't the first time. But I decided it was a good laugh and went back again."

"And . . .?"

"And I clobbered a taxi as I pulled out. I almost got away but some blasted off-duty cop just happened to be walking past and bingo, that's me collared."

"Don't you two ever stop talking?"

They were interrupted by Jacko appearing behind them.

"Sorry, Jacko, he wanted to know about the Roller story."

"Oh yes, good story that. Pity you got nicked, wasn't it. Still, you all do, don't you. Otherwise I wouldn't have to be here."

Lol was surprised. It was the first time he had heard any adult make what could pass for a joke about nicking cars.

By the time Jacko told them all they could go, Lol was tired, his back muscles aching from bending over so much, but he felt good. Really good.

He pulled on his anorak and called out goodbye to Biffo.

"Oi! Where the hell do you think you're going?" Lol swung round to see Biffo, one hip raised, slowly tapping a long metal spanner into the palm of his hand.

"I thought Jacko said we could go."

"Yeah, well, he meant we can go when we've cleaned up. Look, man, let's get one thing straight. You and me's a team now. I didn't have much say about it but we're a team and that means if anything goes wrong we both get it — see?"

Lol got the point all right but he still couldn't make out what had suddenly made Biffo so angry. A few tools left out? He was as bad as his mother moaning about the state of his bedroom.

"So?"

"So all the tools in this box were issued

to our team and if anything's missing we carry the can," Biffo told him. "So how about making sure that everything goes back in the box instead of racing off like it's school and the bell for playtime just went."

Lol bit back his anger. He wanted to go and punch that stupid black face but knew that Jacko would come in and he'd end up in trouble. Anyway, he thought ruefully, Biffo looked more than capable of taking care of himself, spanner or no spanner.

Together they carefully cleaned the tools, counted them and put them in the box. Then they wiped their hands and turned to go.

"Lol, can I have a word with you?" Jacko's voice stopped Lol in his tracks. Biffo continued walking then turned back just as he went through the garage door.

"You're going to get those nice jeans real filthy in no time," he scoffed. "I'll bring you my spare overalls if you like — now we're a team."

"Thanks, Biffo, and I'll bring something to eat during the break."

"Was it as bad as you thought it was going to be?" Jacko asked when Biffo had disappeared out of earshot. Lol shook his head.

"Any questions before you zoom off?"

Lol fidgeted, shoes scuffing the rough ground, hands twisting at his side.

"Come on," Jacko prompted. "I can

only say no, or at worst give you a good clip round the ear for cheek."

"Er, well, I was wondering," Lol stuttered lamely, "I wanted to know when do we get to do some driving?" Finally he blurted it all out in a rush, then was silent.

Jacko looked at him. "Good question. Actually most of the lads who come here ask that question in the first half hour."

"And?"

"And the answer is simple. The only car for you all to drive at the moment is Bessie and at the moment Bessie won't go anywhere however much you want her to. A big problem here, as in most places, is money. We can only afford a limited number of parts, even secondhand ones." He caught sight of Lol's downcast face and added: "Still, we should manage something soon, particularly now we have your genius to help us," and he winked. "Right, off you go. Goodbye, Lol."

"Goodbye Mr Jack . . . Jacko," he quickly corrected himself.

When he arrived home the curtains were drawn and the light shone dimly through them. He ran up the drive and burst through the kitchen door taking his mother in his arms and whirling her about.

"Laurence, Laurence, you're going to make me drop the saucepan," she laughed as she struggled to shake off his grip. "I take it everything went okay."

"Uuum, it was . . . all right," he tried to sound casual. Then, catching his mother's eye added: "No seriously, Mum, it was good. I liked it."

The sound of the back door opening broke the silence between them. Lol's father strode into the kitchen followed by a puffing Rocket.

"You're back late," he said, bending down to take off the dog's lead.

"I walked. Next time I'll take the bike," Lol said.

"How did it go?"

Lol was not going to get away with just an "O.K." Slowly, tortuously at first, then more cheerfully and with enthusiasm Lol told him about the Project, about Jacko and the others.

"That — what did you call him, Bimbo — he sounds nice," his mother said.

"Biffo," Lol corrected her. "Yes, he's O.K."

"The man who invented the word 'O.K.' should be shot," his father complained but he was smiling. It was the easiest meal the three of them had eaten in a long time. Lol was amazed to discover that his father had once worked in a garage.

"I was rather good," his father boasted cheerfully. "Wait a minute," and he suddenly leapt up, his meal half-eaten, and went to one of the cupboards.

Lol and his mother looked at each other

in amazement as the contents of the cupboard were deposited on the floor as the search continued.

"What on earth is he doing?" Lol's mother got up to put his father's plate back in the oven to keep warm.

Lol shook his head. He was baffled. He'd never seen anything like it. Usually his father went mad at any interruption at mealtimes.

"There we are, I knew it was in there somewhere." His father sank back on his heels and pushed all the things he had taken out of the cupboard back in an untidy muddle.

"You might find this quite useful," he said as he handed Lol a large hard-backed book. "Where's my dinner gone?"

"Thanks, Dad." Lol looked at the book. On the front was a colour picture of a car and the headline written in white letters now rather dingy with age — "The Motor Car."

"I bought it ages ago when I did bits and pieces on the car. I dare say things have changed a bit but if your banger's as old as I guess it is, you'll probably find all you need in there."

Although at first the diagrams made no sense to him, slowly, under the careful tuition of Jacko, he became adept at coping with the intricacies of car engines.

Gradually he came to live for Bessie and bangers. At night he dreamt about banger racing. He would be there, tearing around the track, carefully coaxing Bessie to give her best, ruthlessly crashing aside anyone who dared get in his way. Finally, with no one else in sight, he passed the chequered flag — he had won. Cheers engulfed the track, someone was trying to talk to him, a newspaper reporter perhaps?

"Laurence, you're going to be late for school again if you don't hurry up."

"School?" Lol leaned up on his pillow. So it had all been a dream. Thank goodness Bessie was real and she would be winning . . . soon. They had been making good progress with her and he was looking forward to that evening's session.

He raced to the bathroom, washed, dressed and bounded down the stairs. He grabbed a piece of toast as he rushed like a whirlwind through the kitchen.

"Laurence, you're going to get indigestion unless you sit down and eat properly," his mother rebuked him. He gave her a kiss, leaving crumbs on her cheek, then mounted his bike and pedalled cheerfully off.

The day dragged, but he perked up when they began studying the internal combustion engine in the physics lesson, and he was engrossed in his diagrams when the buzzer for home time sounded. He walked out to the bike shed with a group of his classmates. They were all laughing and joking about the Geography teacher's new moustache.

"It makes him look like Charlie Chaplin," said one boy.

"More like Adolf Hitler," replied Lol and they burst out laughing again. But as they turned the corner of the bike shed, the laughing stopped completely. A group of boys in leather jackets were leaning against the rail, cigarettes hanging from their lips. Lol felt his stomach sink but it was too late to avoid them.

"Lol," a tall boy with greasy, shoulder-length hair greeted him. "Just the person we're looking for."

"What do you want, Baz?" said Lol, bending to undo the heavy chain from around the front wheel of his bike. All the other boys had drifted away. They could smell trouble in the air.

"Now, is that the way for you to talk to an old friend?" the boy said, leaning forward and taking hold of Lol's school blazer by the lapels.

"We get the distinct impression that you're avoiding us, and we don't think that's very friendly at all," he said menacingly.

Lol straightened up and pushed the other boy's hands from his coat.

"If you get the impression that I'm avoiding you, you are more intelligent than I gave you credit for." Later, he was amazed at what he had said, the words just seemed to flow out.

The group of boys looked at one

another, eyebrows raised. Baz stepped forward again.

"Now that's not exactly polite is it," he said, pushing Lol backwards with small taps on one shoulder then the other. "Not the way to treat friends at all."

"Friends?" Lol spat out the words, all the anger of the last few months spilling out. "Friends? What kind of flaming friends are you? Friends don't run off and leave someone else to carry the can. Friends stand by you. Friends? Huh, I'd feel more at home with a rattlesnake than with you lot."

The boys looked surprised. They had never heard Lol so angry, yet so in control of himself.

"Just remember," said Baz, "you're *our* friend and that means helping us out when we need it."

He turned back to his friends and Lol began to relax. Empty threats. Then suddenly Baz whirled round and punched Lol hard in the stomach, making him sink to his knees in agony.

"We'll be calling you . . . friend," Baz laughed as he and his mates ran off.

Lol slumped to the floor holding his stomach. Try as he might, he could not stop the tears springing to his eyes. Thank goodness everyone else had long gone. He sat on the cold concrete floor for several minutes before trying to stand up, breathing in short shallow breaths as the pain from his bruised stomach slowly subsided. He pulled his bike from the rack, slowly got on to it, and pedalled off.

He weaved along the road as he tried to ride the bike with one hand on the handlebars, the other pressed against his stomach. He turned to go over the railway bridge and headed straight towards the Project. Hopefully no one else would have arrived yet and he would have time to recover.

He winced as he rode along the pot-holed lane. Carefully he dismounted and went into the garage. There was no one else about and he sat down on some sacks, head bent forward on to his knees, both arms wrapped around his stomach.

"Hey, are you O.K?" The voice made him start, sending little waves of pain flooding through his body. He looked all round the garage but still couldn't see anyone.

"You look absolutely awful. Want a cup of tea?"

Lol turned and saw a small thin figure wearing overalls standing by the door that joined the two garages.

"Oh it's you." He relaxed back against the sacks. It was Gill, Jacko's daughter. She often came in while the boys were working and sometimes would make them all tea. He had always thought it rather odd that a girl should be so interested in cars but they had got used to her.

"What's up with you, did you come off your bike?"

He laughed. If only that were it.

"Are you hurt?" He found the anxiety in her voice strangely reassuring.

"Only when I laugh."

As the kettle boiled she carefully filled two mugs, dunking the teabags with a screwdriver and shovelling in heaped teaspoons of sugar.

"You won't mention this to anyone, will you?" he asked her, hoping his voice sounded casual, when she handed him the steaming mug.

"I still don't really know what happened so how can I tell anyone?" she answered logically, and he felt relieved.

They sat talking together until the first of the other boys arrived. Then Lol jumped up and began to put on his overalls, but not before Biffo had caught his eye and given him a big wink.

"You'd better watch out," he said grinning. "If Jacko catches you trying to get well in with the management's daughter you're in big trouble."

To his annoyance Lol felt himself going red.

Chapter Three

The boys were just getting going on their work when Jacko walked in. He picked up a big spanner and beat it against an old wheel hub that was lying on the bench.

"O.K. you lot," he shouted, trying to make himself heard above the din. "Let's have some silence for a few minutes. I've got some news that might interest you."

The boys stopped work and gathered around him, eager to find out what news could have made him look so pleased.

"This morning I got a letter from the Banger Racing Association." There was a murmur of interest from the boys.

"Anyway," Jacko raised his voice, "they have decided to hold a special junior banger racing championship, just a one-day knock-out event, and they want to know if we'd like to enter."

The din was deafening. All the boys

were talking at once, asking questions, clapping each other on the shoulders, laughing and joking.

"There will be a cash prize and . . ." again he had to wait for the cheering to stop, "the whole thing is to be televised."

This time, Jacko had to wait several minutes before he could continue.

"Hold it, hold it," he eventually silenced them. "That was the good news . . ."

"I knew it," Biffo, face downcast, interrupted.

"As I said, that was the good news. The bad news is that we have very little money to spend on Bessie. I have already been in touch with the local authority for some more — but they say there isn't any." There was a sarcastic laugh from the boys.

"Perhaps Mr Mayor could spare us just a little bit from his pocket money," said Biffo, adopting a "little boy" look.

"Very funny," said Jacko. "Actually, I've already asked him and he says he needs it all for his sherbet dabs. Seriously, I think we have just about enough bits and pieces around the place to get Bessie running adequately. But that's about it. There'll be nothing left over for extras."

"Jacko?" It was Lol who spoke. "Where are we going to practise with Bessie? I mean, surely we can't go out there on to the track without any proper practice? We won't stand a chance."

"You're right, and I am working on it. Now, may I suggest that perhaps we had better spend some time on persuading Bessie to move at all, never mind win races."

They all worked on late into the night. For most of the time the garage was quiet except for a gentle murmur of voices and the clink of tools on metal. Once, Gill appeared with mugs of tea on a tray and a plate of biscuits and the boys stopped for a ten-minute break but they needed no persuasion to return to their jobs.

By home time, although there was very little difference about the way Bessie looked, the boys knew that she was not just the wreck she seemed.

The engine, which had been belching heavy black smoke, now puttered and spluttered but the exhaust was clean.

Everyone stood back admiringly as Alan gunned the accelerator, making the engine roar.

"I think we might just have time to take her for a little stroll." Jacko began to pull open the large garage doors. He flicked a light switch and two powerful beams flooded the track between the garage and Jacko's house.

Cautiously, with shouted advice from the other boys, Alan reversed Bessie out.

Outside, there was an anxious silence as Bessie's engine suddenly died. Alan leaned forward and turned the key — a splutter then silence. An air of doom hung over the little group gathered in the garage doorway. Jacko went over to the driver's side and, after a quick conversation, Alan leaned forward and turned the key again. Again there was a spluttering, but gradually the roar grew louder and louder.

"Take her down the lane," Jacko told Alan, and with a little leap that set the boys jeering, Bessie moved off. When she returned Jacko told them to take one turn each and, before anyone else could move, like a little monkey Biffo had slipped through the open window and was fastening himself in. The doors were tied shut but before she was raced they would be welded so they did not spring open if she were hit.

The boys jostled to be next to drive. The thought of getting behind the wheel of a car legally, even for such a sedate drive, was a treat no one wanted to miss.

"Don't fight," Jacko told them. "I think there's just enough time for everyone to have a quick go. Anyway, there's always Saturday."

But Saturday wasn't good enough for the impatient youngsters, and one by one they slid into the driver's seat. None managed to go more than about five miles an hour but it was a treat they relished. Finally, Bessie was driven back into the garage and the tools were hurriedly packed away.

As Lol went to get his bike Gill appeared beside him.

"How's the stomach?" she asked.

"*Shush.*" The last thing he wanted was for any of the others to find out about it.

"I don't see why it's got to be such a secret."

"Because it's nobody's business but mine. I can handle it."

She shrugged. "O.K., if that's the way you want it."

"Hey, Lol!" A panting Biffo ran up behind him as he wheeled the bike along the now dark track to the lane. "Hang on a minute, wait for me."

Lol stopped. "You should quit smoking, then you wouldn't be so out of condition."

"Me? Out of condition? I'm the fittest thing in our street. When my mum goes after me she doesn't stand a chance. *Whoosh*, that's me away, man."

"You getting the bus?" Lol knew that sometimes Biffo walked home, preferring to pocket the money his mother gave him for the fares.

"No, I'm saving."

"For what?"

"Here, take a look at this," Biffo pulled a section of the local newspaper out of his pocket. Lol halted under a lamp post so he could see properly.

"Banger Racing, Red Ash Stadium, Saturday," he read it aloud. "Fantastic. Are you going?"

"Oh no, I'm just carrying that around

in case anyone stops me in the street and asks me. 'Course I'm going. You want to come too?"

Lol considered. "How much?"

"Entrance money is £1.50 and we'll need about a quid to get there and back."

To Lol that was a fortune. All his pocket money went towards paying off his fine. But it was too good an opportunity to miss. He'd just have to get the money somehow.

"O.K. How will we get away from the Project in time to see the races?"

Biffo winked. "Leave it to me. I'll ask Jacko. You can come back to my place afterwards if you like," Biffo called to him as he pedalled off.

"Great, thanks."

Lol was still thinking about how he could get the money when he got home. He put the bike away in the shed and went inside. The kitchen was in darkness but he could hear the television on in the other room. He looked in the fridge and found a plate of sandwiches — ham, his favourite — and poured himself a glass of milk.

"Minder" was on the TV, and his parents looked up when he entered then quickly turned back to the screen. He sat down beside his father on the sofa and began eating his tea. Rocket got up from his usual spot in front of the fire and began a long vigil by Lol's knee, ready to snap up any titbits that might "accidentally" fall.

"Had a good evening, love?" his mother asked when the programme had finally ended.

"O.K."

"How's that old banger — what's her name . . .?"

"Bessie."

"That's it, Bessie. How's she getting along?"

"O.K., but she needs a lot of work still. Guess what?" He didn't wait for their response. "We've been invited to take part in a banger championship. To go on telly."

"When's that?" His father looked over his newspaper.

"Next month some time."

"Are you driving? It's quite an art, you know, driving around a track with all those others trying to push you off."

"It hasn't been decided yet. We're going to have trials and the best one gets to drive."

His father put his paper down on his knee and sat, silently thinking.

"Do you know, I believe I saw something in yesterday's paper about banger racing. . . ." He got up and went to forage amongst some papers stacked on a chair.

"Here it is. Banger racing, Red Ash Stadium, Saturday. You should go along, it will give you some idea of what it's all about."

Lol felt as if he was hearing things.

"I wouldn't mind going with you . . . ." His hopes dived again — what would Biffo say if he dragged his father along — ". . . but I've got to do an extra shift on Saturday, Fred Johnson fell and broke his leg. He's in hospital."

"Oh what a shame, dear," Lol's mother interrupted. "He's such a nice man. How did he manage to fall?"

The conversation then veered dramatically away from bangers and Lol realized the moment to mention money was lost. He went to bed still no nearer having any idea of how he was going to be able to afford to go.

The next morning after he had eaten his breakfast he went into the sitting room to find the newspaper advertisement about the race. The paper was still on the settee where his father had left it.

As he sat reading the ad that he now knew almost word perfectly, he caught sight of his mother's handbag, open by the chair. Lol quickly looked away, feeling guiltily that even to think of taking the money was almost as bad as actually pocketing it.

But he couldn't keep his eyes off the purse, tucked away with the other contents of the bag.

Bending down, he flicked the catch and the purse opened. The inside was full of pound notes and coins. It was shopping day — she wouldn't miss a couple of quid.

She'd just think she'd spent more than she had.

It was easy. So easy. Just take a couple of pounds. Now, quickly, before someone comes. His hand hovered away from the newspaper then quickly returned to his lap. The coins seemed to taunt him.

The bang of a door made Lol jump inches off the settee. Quickly he leapt up and was standing, paper crushed in his hands, when his father walked in.

"Laurence, I've been thinking. I know you can't have any money — what with the fine and everything — so I thought you could use this to go banger racing. It's a good cause after all." Then, almost as if he was embarrassed by his good intentions, he hastily retreated.

Lol stared down at the three pounds in his hand. He went red and felt hot all over. He flicked a guilty glance down at the bag. Would he have taken the money if his father had not come in? He realized he really didn't know and he too hurried from the room as if glad to escape the temptation.

That Saturday, he and Biffo went together to ask Jacko if they could leave earlier than usual, and he immediately agreed.

"I just wish I could come with you," he said. "But some of us have to stay around and work."

"Can I come?" Gill, at work on the bench beside them had overheard the conversation. Biffo and Lol looked at each other, then at her.

"Go on," she pleaded. "I can pay my own way."

Biffo shrugged. "Why not? I guess so." Though he sounded decidedly reluctant Gill didn't care.

"Great," she said ecstatically, returning to her work.

"Thanks, lads," said Jacko, when they had moved out of Gill's earshot. "I hope she won't be a nuisance."

"What d'you want to invite her for?" snapped Lol when he and Biffo were alone.

"Hey, man, and tell me how I could have got out of it with her old man listening? Anyway, I thought she was your little fancy?"

"I hardly know her. I can't help it if she follows me around. This afternoon is going to be a disaster, I just know it is." Sulkily he crouched down and pulled himself under the car.

At first, Lol thought they might escape without Gill. When they put away their tools and put on their anoraks she was nowhere to be seen. But as they left the garage she came running up the track.

"Hey, you weren't going off without me, were you?" She said it with a laugh but eyed them severely.

" 'Course not," Biffo reassured her while Lol, hands thrust deep into coat pockets, hurried off ahead of them.

By the time they got to the stadium there were crowds of people milling about.

"Let's sneak round to the car park and see them getting the cars ready," Biffo suggested.

"We won't miss any of the races will we?" Lol was anxious not to miss a second of this supreme treat.

"No, don't worry. They'll make an announcement when they're ready and we'll have loads of time to go inside."

Although out of bounds, it was not hard to get into the car park. They just waited until the uniformed guard was showing a car and trailer which way to go, then slipped in, using the high-sided trailer for cover.

The car park was like a dream world. Everywhere there were bangers. Some were quite smart and new, others in advanced stages of falling apart but still being tended lovingly by their crews.

Lol was impressed with some of the set-ups — proper trailers, team uniforms, even large caravans so the drivers and mechanics could take a tea break or just get out of the icy wind.

But it was the actual cars that fascinated him most. The majority had their bonnets up getting last-minute tunings, and he leaned over, enviously watching the powerful engines.

Although he got shooed away a couple of times, most of the drivers were only too happy to have someone — obviously an admirer — watch them work.

"Hiya kid — you racing?" A grease-smeared face appeared from the other side of the yawning bonnet.

"Wish I was," Lol told him self-consciously.

"No car?" The man was wiping his hands on his already dirt-encrusted over-alls.

"Yes, I've got a car," Lol carefully left out the rest of the details. "But she's not running properly yet. We're still working on her."

"What kind?"

"Vanguard."

The man nodded knowledgeably. "Nice sturdy car, should do all right for you. Your dad drive it?"

"No," Lol told him hurriedly. "He isn't really interested in bangers. It's . . . it's a group of my mates. We're all doing it together."

"That's the way, spread the cost around. Costs me an arm and a leg to keep this heap going." He gave his car an affectionate knock on the front wing.

"Fancy getting in and starting her up?"

"Me?"

"Yes — if you don't mind. Then I can see if I've fixed the leak. Just one turn of the key, no choke, one blast on the accelerator, then let it idle. O.K?"

"You bet." Lol levered himself through

the window before the man could change his mind. He settled himself in the seat. It was a bit big for him but it felt good.

"Ready?" he called out.

"Ready. Fire away."

Lol turned the key and the engine roared briefly into life. He pushed his foot down on the accelerator then released it. With a gurgle and a metallic rumble the engine died away.

"Don't worry." The man came round and put his head through the open window. "It often does that. Most people don't manage to get it going at all. Try again."

Lol did and this time the engine roared with a satisfying regularity.

"How is it?" he shouted out of the window.

"Seems O.K. Thanks. You can turn it off now."

Reluctantly, Lol turned the ignition off and pulled himself out of the car. As he went round to the front, Biffo walked up.

"Hiya, what you up to?"

"He's been giving me a hand," the man told him. "My name's Charlie Gibson by the way and you're . . .?"

"Laurence Lord, but everyone calls me Lol."

"Biffo they call me," Biffo said. He was silent for a few minutes and Lol was a little embarrassed at the unerring stare he fixed on his new friend.

"Say, are you *the* Charlie Gibson?"

The man laughed. "Now, I don't know about that. It depends on who *the* Charlie Gibson is."

"The stock-car racer. You won the championship last year, didn't you?"

"You've got a good memory. Do you follow stock cars?"

"Only in the magazines. I can't afford to go to races since they shut down the track near here. I saw an article about you in this month's magazine. It said you'd retired."

"Yeah, well I suppose I have really. It takes up a lot of time — and money. I own my own business and I've been really neglecting it over the last few years. It's not fair on the wife."

"Won't you miss it?" Lol could not imagine anyone who had been so good just giving it all up — and for work!

"I'll still do the odd bit — like this old banger — but the only way to get on in stocks is taking part regularly. You can't afford to do it piecemeal."

With a loud crackle, they were interrupted by the loud-speakers bursting into life.

"Contestants for the first race please make their way to the entrance tunnel. Contestants for the first race please make their way to the entrance tunnel."

"Right, that's me," Charlie told them and closed the bonnet with a bang. While Lol and Biffo watched, he went to his car and took out a red helmet with a white stripe down the side and the word GIBSON neatly printed on the front.

"You two going to be here until the end?" he asked as he did up the chin strap.

Both nodded.

"Fancy giving me a hand getting this back on the trailer after the races are over? Usually a friend helps me, but he couldn't make it this week."

"You bet," Lol told him enthusiastically.

"Right. Show the guy on the gate this," and he handed over a small white cardboard ticket with the words "Pit Pass" printed on. "Now I'd better be going."

The boys stood clear as he expertly swung himself into the car, then settled himself in the seat and did up the two large safety straps that came over his shoulders and pinned him to the seat.

He leaned forward, and in a second the car burst noisily into life. Finally, with a little thumbs up at them, he drove the car slowly towards the place where a line was forming outside the entrance to the track.

"Come on," Lol told Biffo and they ran towards the public entrance. When they got close they could see Gill nervously scanning the approaching faces.

"Where on earth have you been?" she said to them angrily as they joined her and filed in to take up their seats. "I'd given you up for lost."

"Oh, stop moaning. We're here now."

They had just got in their seats when a great roar went up from the crowd and the bangers made their way on to the ash perimeter track.

Altogether there were eight cars and the air was heavy with noise as engines were revved frantically. Acrid exhaust fumes floated upwards and hung like a pall over the whole stadium.

A loud hooter sounded and the cars drew up in four untidy lines of two abreast. Charlie was on the outside in the second row.

The hooter sounded again, twice, and with a sound of engines that completely drowned out the cheering, the bangers moved off.

Lol laughed and pointed to the end car. Whilst the others had moved off with a rush, it had gone precisely nowhere. Now the driver was frantically gesturing to officials, who were running to push him off the track.

They just made it. Scarcely had they pushed the car into the centre when the first of the other bangers went past. To their disappointment Lol and Biffo saw that Charlie was lying in fourth place. The leader was a large red car with 77 painted in white on the side.

The next casualty was the car lying in third place, which tried to cut a corner too tight and was crushed into the barriers. Another cheer went up as they watched the driver pull himself clear and hitch a lift on the marshall's car.

"Look!" Biffo yelled, pointing down at the track. Lol felt a thrill as he saw Charlie's car ram the second-placed one and send it spinning. The car made its way back onto the track, but Charlie had raced on and was now challenging the leader.

"Come on, Charlie!" Lol bellowed as the excitement took him over. "Come on, Charlie!"

By now the track was strewn with the debris of dead cars. Only four were still running and one of those had got steam billowing in an angry plume from the bonnet.

As they went into the final turn, the longest section of the track, Charlie and the leading car were neck and neck. Then, just when it seemed he had lost, the other car faded and slowed until it could barely crawl over the line.

They saw a triumphant fist come out of the open window as Charlie roared across the line. The hooter sounded — and he had won.

"Not bad," Biffo said, sitting down again.

"Not bad! Flippin' brilliant," Lol enthused as he watched those cars that could move drive off the track. Then the repair truck — a huge tank of a vehicle — came and dragged off the wrecks.

In all there were eight races during the afternoon, and when the final one was completed, the centre of the track was littered with old tyres and bits of metal that had fallen, or been knocked off. Slowly people began to file out and make their way home.

"Where are you going?" Gill wanted to know when, at the exit, Lol and Biffo turned to go back to the car park.

They looked at each other. The last thing they wanted was her hanging onto their coat tails.

"We just thought we'd go and see them loading the cars up. It won't be very interesting, Gill."

"It's all right. It sounds fun."

"What time does your father expect you home? You don't want to be late," Biffo asked hopefully.

"Oh, anytime's O.K. with him." She passed them, leading the way through the steady stream of spectators.

In the end, they didn't need the pit pass. The guard was more interested in ushering the cars away than keeping them out. They found Charlie hammering away at his car with a huge sledgehammer, trying to knock two deep dents out of the wing.

"Hello there," he looked up as they stopped to watch.

"Congratulations," Lol said, and Charlie laughed.

"Yeah, not bad first time out, is it? Well," and he broke off as he saw Gill. "And how are you, young Gill?"

Lol's jaw dropped as Charlie and Gill

talked like old friends. Seeing his face, Charlie explained: "I used to race with Gill's father, but she was a whole lot smaller then. We used to pile up four tyres and pop her in the middle. She couldn't get into mischief then!"

"I'd forgotten about that," she told him in mock anger. "You were both really mean."

With Lol steering, and Charlie, Biffo and Gill pushing, they managed to get the banger onto the trailer quite easily. As Charlie put up the end of the trailer ramps, the others secured the banger with ropes.

"Thanks," Charlie told them when they had finished clearing up. "Can I give you a lift anywhere — I'm going towards the motorway."

"No, it's O.K. thanks," Lol told him, though he would have liked to have had the chance of talking to him further. "We get the bus and it goes the other way."

"Coming to the next meet?"

"If we can." Lol would have enjoyed nothing more. "Can we come round the back to help you again?"

"Of course. Tell you what. Perhaps I could come over and give you a hand with your banger some time. Gill's got my number."

"That would be great. Thanks."

The three of them stood, waving once

or twice, until Charlie's car and trailer disappeared out of the car park and out of sight.

Chapter Four

During the following weeks, Lol spent almost every spare moment at the Project and, when he wasn't there, he was thinking about it. Cars and engines became the most important thing in his life.

The change in Bessie was staggering. Her engine, while not exactly smooth, rumbled and roared quite satisfactorily. All surplus pieces, like wing mirrors, door handles and wheel hubs, had been removed from the exterior, heavy metal bashers rather than bumpers had been welded into place and a reinforced webbing harness had been carefully fitted to the driver's seat.

Now when the boys looked at Bessie they saw not just a loved wreck of a car. They saw a *banger*.

Whenever they could, the boys would take her out and drive down the long track, building up enough speed to do flashy hand brake turns on the gravel parking place outside Jacko's house. All of them wanted to drive her all of the time, so a complicated system was worked out according to how much work they did on her, punctuality, and how well behaved they were at the Project.

There had been alarm when it was discovered that John, who had been responsible for much of the more complicated mechanical work, had served his full 250 hours at the Project. John had calmly accepted his fate, but the others presented a noisy attack and it was agreed that he could still keep coming, at least until another boy was allocated his place.

"It's not that we want to get rid of John," Jacko had tried to explain to the other boys when the noisy deputation reached him. "But you must see that there are very few facilities like this in the whole country, never mind in this area. . . ."

"So now he's just chucked out like an old rag," Alan scowled.

"Hardly that. And he has got the chance of a good apprenticeship on the strength of his work here. Anyway, there's nothing to stop you lot getting together and starting your own club once your time here is over," he told them.

"You'd help us?" Alan asked him.

"As much as I could. But don't forget

most of my time is taken up here. It *is* my job."

They stared at him, a miserable semicircle of silence. Even Lol, the newest arrival, realized it would not be long before he too had to stop going. Then what? He had come to depend on the Project for his interest — and his friends.

"Tell you what," Jacko chewed on his fingers for a few moments, deep in thought. "There's cash prizes in this contest, right?"

"Right."

"What would you say if I ask the local authority if the money — should you win — could go to the setting up of a Banger Club? A sort of progression from here. What about it?"

A great cheer of enthusiasm went up. They jumped around clapping him on the back, and picking each other up in huge bear hugs.

"So who's going to drive Bessie and win all this money for us?" Biffo's voice, loud and determined, brought silence.

"Oh yes, I was going to tell you about that . . . I've got permission from the council to use that piece of scrap land behind my house for one day as a track. That way, we won't have any problem about transporting Bessie, as she hasn't any road tax.

"On Saturday, we'll mark out a course. Everyone can do a couple of laps then we'll all vote on who we think has the most potential. How does that sound?"

The boys looked at each other then all agreed. That seemed the fairest way, and there was also the bonus that at least everyone would get the chance of a really good blast in her — win or lose.

Later, as Biffo and Lol walked away from the Project they speculated about Saturday's trials.

"Who do you think will win?" Biffo asked Lol.

"Well, you've got a good chance," Lol told him loyally, "though from what I hear Zac's pretty good. He never got caught driving the cars, only afterwards, because he used to leave them somewhere stupid and get spotted running off."

"What about you?" Lol knew that Biffo was taunting him. He had never been exactly modest about his driving skills.

"I've as good a chance as any, I guess. I really fancy the idea of a banger club, don't you? Even if we only get third prize there'd still be enough money to buy something and we could get Charlie along to give us some tips."

"Yeah. We could get in the league. Bessie II."

At the crossroads they parted.

"See ya," Lol called, half turning in the saddle.

"May the best man win," shouted Biffo.

"I will," Lol's voice echoed back to him.

The rest of the week seemed to take forever, but at last Saturday dawned bright and sunny after a week of almost non-stop rain and drizzle.

Lol raced down the stairs. In spite of his anxiety he had overslept. Now he wouldn't even have time for breakfast. When he appeared in the kitchen his father was seated, gently caressing Rocket's ears. Lol could sense the tension in the air.

"Hi" he said, reaching for a slice of toast to take with him.

"What's this?" asked his father suddenly, tossing a grey schoolbook across the table.

"My maths book," replied Lol, silently cursing himself for not keeping it out of sight. Now he knew what was coming.

"Yes I can see it's a maths book," said his father. "What I meant was, what's this?" He pointed to the pattern of red crosses that marked the page. "And this?" He indicated more crosses and seven or eight lines of writing at the end of the figures.

"Wrong. Every one of them is wrong, for pages and pages. And according to what your teacher has written there is plenty of work missing too. Well?" He stared at Lol who gazed intently at his toast.

"This has got to stop. You spend all your time down with that stupid car. It's all you ever think about. Well, I won't stand for it. Your schoolwork comes first."

Lol went bright red and hung his head even lower.

"Are you listening to a single word I'm saying?" his father shouted at him. "That place is supposed to help you, not ruin your school work. I just can't believe that any son of mine is going to flunk out of school without even one exam. You're not stupid; you just don't work."

"I do work," Lol, almost uncontrollable with anger, virtually screamed. "I work really hard at the Project. I learn things, really important things, but you don't care, do you. Because you can't boast about it, because you can't say I'm top of the class, it's wrong, isn't it? Nothing I do is right — ever."

And with that he stormed from the room, hurling the door shut behind him and snatching his bike from the shed. He sped off towards the Project, his anger seething and growing with each swing of the pedals. When he eventually arrived he was still red and angry.

"Where on earth have you been?" said Biffo as Lol cycled round the side of Jacko's house towards the waste ground. "It's your turn next, we drew lots. Don't you want to drive? You chicken or something?"

He was grinning, but Lol pushed past him without answering. He took the white helmet that lay on Bessie's bonnet and swung himself into the car. He wriggled into the narrow seat. It fitted like a glove and the tight safety harness held him firmly.

Turning the ignition switch he pressed the accelerator again and again until the roar of the engine was deafening and huge clouds of dirty smoke poured from her exhaust.

"Hold it, hold it," Jacko shouted above the din, "there's no need to try for a vertical take-off. I want you to take it steady. What we want is three circuits — gentle circuits — to give us a good idea of how you handle her. Watch out for that top corner, there isn't much room to squeeze past the wall. And Lol — don't prang her, we haven't got enough money for a new spark plug, never mind anything else."

Lol gave a curt nod of his head then jammed Bessie into gear, spraying a jet of soil and grass behind him as her wheels struggled to find a hold on the slippery surface. His hands clenched the steering wheel until the knuckles began to go white, and his foot went harder and harder down on the accelerator. He slid into the first bend, expertly corrected it and straightened up for the long stretch. He pumped the accelerator again and slid into the second bend.

He'd show them, he'd show them he could be good at something. Stupid car! Huh, Bessie was the greatest. Together he and Bessie were unbeatable.

Biffo and the rest of the boys, standing

on a small ridge, were amazed.

"What the hell's he playing at?" shouted Jacko. "I told him to take it steady. Anyone would think this was the Championship. I hope he realizes just how slippery the ground is."

Almost as he spoke Bessie slewed into the top curve. Inside, Lol struggled to straighten her. The stomach-churning slithering had brought him back to reality with a jolt. His hands swung the wheel from one side to the other, trying to get her to ride out the slide but now she was going sideways, out of control, carried along by her own weight.

Suddenly there was a sickening crunch and Bessie stopped, impaled on an old stone trough sticking out of the wall.

The force of the crash threw Lol full weight against his harness and momentarily he was winded. He raised his head slowly and looked around him. It was like slow motion. He could see Jacko and the others racing across the field towards him. Slowly, with shaking hands, he unbuckled the harness and, taking hold of the roof edge, pulled himself clear.

"Are you all right?" Jacko held him, strong arms on his shoulders, virtually holding him up. Then, as he realized Lol was unhurt, his concern turned to anger.

"What the devil were you playing at? I told you to take it easy."

The other boys were grouped around Bessie, anxiously peering under her to see the extent of the damage.

"Looks like the back axle." John, who had been under the car, shook his head miserably.

"You maniac," Biffo screamed angrily at Lol. "You've wrecked her. You had to show off, didn't you? You had to show you're such a damned good driver. So smart. Now she's wrecked and no one gets the chance to race her. We're out of the championship before we even started." He lunged towards Lol, fists raised, but Jacko caught hold of him and pushed him back.

"I should beat your stupid brains in," Biffo continued, struggling against Jacko's hold. "That's if you got any stupid brains at all."

The other boys moved forward towards Lol. It was a solid wall of hate against him.

"Why don't you go drop dead somewhere?" shouted Zac. "We don't want you round here no more."

"That's right, shove off," joined in a couple of the other boys. "And don't come back."

Lol looked at Jacko who took his arm and led him away from the group.

"I think perhaps it might be better if you went home," he told him. "Just give them time to cool off. They'll probably have forgotten about it in a couple of hours."

"But what about Bessie?" The full

impact of what had happened was just beginning to hit him. "Is she badly damaged, will she be O.K. for the race?"

"I'm afraid that's very unlikely," said Jacko gloomily. "If it really is the axle then it's not just the money, though that's bad enough. There just aren't a lot of old Vanguards about, even in the scrap yards. No, I'm afraid we're out of the championships, unless a miracle happens."

Lol started walking back to the garage, pushing his bike before him. He turned and looked at the boys gathering around Jacko as he bent over Bessie. Occasionally one of them would look towards him, hostile and resentful, and Lol looked away quickly.

It had been an accident — couldn't they see that? It could have happened to anyone, he thought to himself. He'd wait until they cooled down a bit then explain. Biffo would understand. They were mates.

He waited round the corner of the garage, out of sight until he could test the temperature of their feelings.

"I'm afraid there's nothing I can do about it, Biffo," Jacko's voice could easily be heard. "That axle's broken. There just isn't enough for a replacement, even if we could find one."

"Hey man, you ain't going to let that maniac get away with it are you? He ain't gonna come here no more, is he?"

"Come on, Biffo, he made a mistake."

"Mistake! Ha. It was our mistake letting him drive poor old Bessie. Now she ain't no good for nothing. Well, if he shows his face round here again I'm gonna smash it."

"Don't be stupid," Jacko's voice had hardened. "You'll do as you're told while you're here. Any trouble, any fighting, and it's you that will be in the hot seat. Got it?"

Biffo was silent for a few moments but Lol could feel the venom even without words.

"Well *I'm* not going to work with him. No way."

They walked off, out of earshot, but Lol didn't need to hear any more. Sneaking a quick look round the corner of the garage to check it was all clear, he got on his bike and cycled away.

He breathed a sigh of relief when he got home and found the house empty. He knew his father would be working and guessed his mother had gone shopping. With any luck she wouldn't be home for hours and he would be spared embarrassing questions about why he was home so early.

He found a can of Coke in the fridge, and picking up the morning paper, went up to his room. The day dragged horribly and when his mother still hadn't returned by four o'clock, he went out on his bike for a ride.

Afterwards, he could not remember where he had been. At the beginning he headed towards the Project, drawn by a macabre curiosity to see them all, but when he got to the top of the lane he decided against it. Maybe Jacko was right. Maybe they just needed time to cool down.

His father's Mini was parked in the drive when he got home, so he carefully cleaned off his bike before putting it away in the shed. He couldn't face any more rows.

Both his parents were sitting watching TV. It was a film, "Bullitt", starring Steve McQueen, and Lol's eyes were riveted to the screen as the star hurled his car through a series of breath-taking stunts.

Suddenly, without a word, his father got up and stepped forward turning the television over to another channel.

"Dad!" Lol wailed noisily.

"Your mother wants to watch Cannon and Ball," he said, flopping back in his seat. "Look, we nearly missed the beginning as it is."

"Doesn't it matter that I wanted to watch the film?"

"When you pay the licence fee and the cost of renting the set, then you can choose the channel," his father said.

Lol sat for a few minutes watching the show. Usually he liked Cannon and Ball but now he found them stupid and not in the least bit funny. He got up.

"Where are you going, dear?" his mother glanced up at him but, before he had a chance to answer, the laughter on the screen drew her attention.

"Up to my room," he said loudly, taking great pleasure in slamming the door as he left.

Upstairs he flung himself down on his bed. He tried to read a book but the words danced in front of his eyes. Even his banger magazine didn't interest him. Finally, boredom forced him to swallow his pride and return downstairs and watch television again.

He was still in a bad temper on Monday when he went for his fortnightly visit to his probation officer.

"How's it going then, Laurence?" Mr Sampson looked across his desk at Lol.

"O.K." Lol hated these "little chats". He could never think of anything to say. Mr Sampson always seemed to know exactly what he had been up to even when he didn't say. It was like being spied on.

He wondered if Jacko had told him about the crash but Mr Sampson made no mention of it.

"Just O.K?"

God, what did he want from him? A two-page essay on how brilliant his life was?

"It's fine. I enjoy it. Thank you." He always felt obliged to tag a "thank you" on to any conversation he had with Mr Sampson.

"Good, Good. Well, Mr Jackson seems to think you are getting along well. Do you get on all right with the other boys?"

Lol was wary. He couldn't make out if Mr Sampson was fishing and did know about the crash and what the boys had said afterwards, or whether it was just a general query.

"Yeah, fine," he muttered, then quickly added, "thank you."

Mr Sampson nodded.

"Right, Laurence. You can go. I'll see you at the usual time. And you know that any problems that you have you can always talk over with me."

"Right. Goodbye." Lol walked to the door before Mr Sampson could think of some reason for keeping him.

Lol spent all of the following Wednesday trying to think up a reason for not going to the Project. It would have to be good to get past his father. In the back of his mind he knew he had to go, that it was part of the court ruling, but he reckoned they couldn't make him go if he was sick — could they?

But his heart sank when he cycled up the drive. Outside was parked a red Cortina — Jacko's car. Presumably he'd come to tell his parents about what had happened the Saturday before. He'd been expecting it, but it still wasn't fair.

Jacko was seated in the kitchen having

a cup of tea with Lol's mum. He could hear their voices as he approached the back door.

"Hello, Lol." Jacko looked up when he entered.

"Hello, love. Mr Jackson was just passing and he dropped in so he could give you a lift. I told him you usually went straight there after school on your bike. Wasn't it lucky you came back today? Have you forgotten something?"

Lol caught Jacko's eye. Why hadn't he told her?

"Yes, I wanted my . . . my magazine. I'll go up and get it." He hurried upstairs and picked up the first magazine he found. Downstairs, Jacko had finished his tea and was waiting for him.

"Goodbye, Mrs Lord, thank you for the tea."

"Goodbye, Mr Jackson, so nice of you to give Laurence a lift. 'Bye, love."

"Why didn't you tell her about last Saturday?" Lol asked him when they were on their way.

"What, the crash? I don't see the point, do you?"

"No." There was more silence. "So why did you come?"

Jacko considered for a few moments, the car cruising easily along the road.

"To be honest, Lol, I thought it might put you off and tempt you to stay away from the Project. And if you did that you would be in trouble with the law. You do realize that, don't you? You have to attend unless I give you permission not to."

"I was coming," Lol said belligerently. "Why shouldn't I? It was an accident. It could have happened to anyone."

When they turned into the drive Lol felt slightly sick, much as he had done when he moved to a new school. He had a fair idea of what would be in store for him. Still, he didn't care. He could cope with whatever they dished out.

Most of the boys had already arrived and were at work on Bessie. No one looked up when he walked in.

"Won't be a tick," said Jacko, hurrying towards the house. "I'll just get changed into my overalls."

"Hey, can anyone smell a funny smell in here?" The voice was Alan's.

"Now you come to mention it, I do smell something funny, like it's gone bad," Biffo replied.

Lol stared at them. He was fighting to control his emotions. He wanted to rush at them but there were too many of them. He knew it would be useless.

He took a deep breath and walked over to Biffo.

"Right. What are we going to do tonight?"

"We? We?" Biffo's voice was high pitched, incredulous. "Well, man, me and Alan here, we're working on the axle. It got broken you know. Some idiot crunched her into a wall."

Lol nodded. So that was the way they were going to play it.

"John?" he asked, turning to the lanky black boy standing watching.

"Me?" he said, surprised. "I'm already fixed up. Zac said he wanted to help me fix the battery terminal leads, didn't you Zac?"

"Sure did."

And so it went on. All the boys teaming up, making it clear that Lol had not been forgiven. He was on his own.

"What's all this hanging around? Hasn't anyone got any work to do?" Jacko marched busily into the garage, familiar blue overalls now zipped into place.

"Lol, you come and give me a hand over here."

They worked quietly together until Gill came in with the tea at seven. At first, the sound of laughter from the other boys had taunted him but gradually he became absorbed in what he and Jacko were doing and he forgot the others . . . almost.

Gill smiled at Lol but, conscious of the others, he barely acknowledged her.

Gill, waiting until her father had gone out, marched over to Biffo.

"For heaven's sake Biffo, he's said he's sorry, what more can he do?"

"Well, well, well. So now you've got a girl to do your talking for you, have you?" Biffo scoffed. "So he's sorry, well big deal. So he damn well should be. He's just a big pain in the backside." Lol turned with fury to Gill. He flung down his mug of tea hearing the crash as the china smashed into a hundred pieces on the stone floor, and without a word he turned on his heel and stormed out.

"Wait — Lol," he heard Gill calling out behind him, but he didn't stop, he didn't even slow down.

"Lol," her voice was a plea. "Where are you going?"

"What's it got to do with you?" he snapped. "Haven't you done enough?"

"But you can't just go. They don't mean anything. They're just a bit angry still about the race."

"Yeah, well maybe I'm angry too. I tried to apologize to them but they won't have it. Good luck to them because I don't care any more. Tell your father I'm ill . . . in fact you can tell him anything you like!" Then, not giving her time to say anything else, he walked quickly out of the gates.

He walked for some time, hands in pockets, head down. He started to go home but realized it was too early. He didn't want to face any probing questions.

A blast on a car horn made him jump and he looked round. A metallic green Capri was drawn up behind him. He took no notice. He didn't know anyone with a car like that — worst luck!

He kept on walking and the horn sounded again. This time the car drew level with him. Slowly the window was wound down and he found himself staring into the grinning faces of Greg and Baz.

Chapter Five

"Hiya Lol, all alonesome," Greg leered at him.

"Wow, what a great car," Lol crouched down on his haunches so his face was on a level with the open window. "Where'd you get it?" His eyes took in the smart leather interior, the sun roof, the cassette player.

"An old mate of mine lent it to me," Baz boasted. "Come on, Lol, we'll give you a lift home."

Lol hesitated. He couldn't believe anyone would lend Baz such a beautiful car. But he pushed the thoughts to the back of his mind. After the taunts of his so-called friends he was pleased that someone was actually seeking his company.

"Come on, make your mind up." Baz revved the car impatiently.

"O.K."

In a second Greg was out and holding forward the seat so Lol could slip into the back. With a whoop Baz gunned the engine and like a rocket the car started.

It was like nothing Lol had ever known before. All the cars hc had ever nicked had been conventional saloon cars, ones he thought would be inconspicuous. Even flat out they couldn't match the effortless speed of this monster.

He settled down against the pale leather seats and luxuriated in the feeling of power.

Although Baz was seventeen and technically old enough to drive, he had never managed to pass his test. Now, he sent the car screaming round corners forcing Lol and Greg to hang on to whatever they could to stop themselves being thrown around the inside.

They raced wildly down Station Road, sending several people on the zebra crossing diving for the pavement.

"Stupid old dodderers," Baz bawled at them nastily. He changed down to go around the roundabout near the park. Once, twice, three times they circled the small grassed oval, the wheels screeching as they painfully fought to hold their grip.

"Round and round and round we go, where we'll stop nobody knows!" Baz was in his element. His eyes were wild with excitement, his gloved hands tight on the steering wheel.

"Baz." Lol struggled to sit up so he could speak to Baz, but the force of the car's speed sent him reeling back.

"Baz," he shouted louder.

"What's up, kid — scared?" He could see Baz's eyes, mocking, staring at him in the mirror.

"Of course not, it's just that I've got to go home. My folks will wonder where I've got to." Already he was regretting ever accepting the lift. Baz and Greg always meant trouble.

"Aw diddums," Greg mocked. "Is his mumsy and dadsy going to be worried when their little lamb doesn't get back on time."

If anything, after that Baz went faster, and Lol began to feel queasy from the violent manoeuvrings. They were almost at the big roundabout before the dual carriageway and Lol knew they had no intention of taking him home. It was in completely the wrong direction.

"Uh, oh." Baz leaned forward to peer intently in the reversing mirror.

"What's up?" Greg turned round to look out of the rear window. "Christ, the police!"

"Oh God," Lol muttered weakly as he too turned to look out of the window. Sure enough, just turning out of a side road, with its blue light already beginning to flash, was a police patrol car. Lol slumped down in the seat, desperate that they should not see him. By automatically doing that he at last admitted to himself that he knew Baz and Greg had stolen the car.

"What are you going to do?" Greg looked across at Baz.

"What am I going to do? I'm going to beat the pants off them, that's what!" Baz boasted. "Hold tight."

They whipped around the roundabout and Lol felt the car slide slightly but then Baz caught it again and with a boost like a rocket they set off.

Lol leaned forward in his seat alternately glancing forward and behind. He watched the speedometer creep up, 160, 180 kph. In the distance, falling farther and farther behind, was the police car. It was only a Mini Metro and it stood little chance against the mighty Capri.

"I told you I'd beat the pants off them," crowed Baz. "Now if I nip down through the estate I'll lose him and then we'll ditch the car. By the time they find it we'll be long gone."

With another screech of tyres he turned off the dual carriageway and down a road that led to the industrial estate.

"Here we go, easy as pie," Baz turned round to laugh at Lol as he curled round a sweeping bend.

"Hey Baz, watch out. That old geezer!" Greg's voice rose to a high-pitched crescendo, but before Lol could see exactly what was happening he heard a thud on the side of the car.

"You've hit him," Greg's voice was shocked and, for a few moments, the car slowed dramatically.

"Silly old geezer, he just stepped out into the road, you saw that." Baz had lost all of his earlier cockiness. "We'd better get the hell out of here," and with that he sent the car racing forward again.

"You've got to stop," Lol protested, looking back at the crumpled figure lying unmoving in the road. "He could be hurt badly. Stop!"

"What, and get nicked by the coppers? You must be mad," Baz shouted at him. "They'll be along soon — too bloody soon — they'll see he's all right."

Lol looked back again but already the body was just a tiny object that could have been anything. They drove the next two or three minutes in silence, then suddenly Baz made a sharp right turn that led to the unfinished car park outside a factory. There were no street lamps. It was the perfect place to dump the car.

"O.K. — let's leg it," he said as he opened the driver's door and got out. Lol pushed the seat forward and holding on to the steering wheel to balance himself, he leapt out too.

"We should go back, to see if he's all right," protested Lol, still thinking of the awful thud as the car had hit the old man.

"Look, you stupid fool!" Baz stood menacingly in front of Lol. "If we go back they'll get us won't they? At the moment they haven't the remotest idea who it was have they?

"So you beat it home, make up whatever story you like about where you've been, but don't mention us," and he pulled Lol towards him until he was eyeball to eyeball. "You got that?"

"Yes," Lol told him, and Baz let go of his anorak. They turned and within seconds were far away, running nimbly over the uneven surface. Lol was suddenly spurred into life too. He had to get away! He took off, running as fast as his legs would carry him. Every second he expected to hear the sound of sirens behind him and he only stopped running when he felt his lungs would burst if he kept it up. He stumbled forward onto the bench by a bus stop and sat, head drooping almost to his knees, sucking in great gulps of breath.

He could feel the blood surging around his head making it pound painfully. His heartbeat was as loud as a clock. His whole body was shaking and he felt sure if he stood up his legs would not support him.

"Are you all right, son?" The voice made him jump, and he swung round, ready to race off. But it was only an elderly couple peering anxiously down at him.

"Me? Oh yes, I'm fine thank you," he said, relief pouring over him. "I just felt a little sick."

"I'd hurry home and go to bed if I were you," the woman said kindly. "Here's your bus now."

Lol looked down the road and saw the swaying red body of the No. 74 coming towards him. He stood up and put out his hand.

"Goodnight son," the couple called to him and, as he boarded the bus, he mumbled an almost inaudible goodnight back.

The bus wound its way at a laboriously slow rate round the estate. There were few people on board, just two young couples and two women who, Lol soon discovered from their conversation, were on their way home from bingo.

"Ooooh look," one of them said suddenly to her friend. "There's been some kind of an accident. There's an ambulance and a police car."

Lol went cold. He didn't want to look but his eyes were drawn automatically to the scene below him. The ambulance men were just shutting the back door and then they raced round to the front. As the ambulance began to move there was a loud bellow as the siren began.

A policeman standing in the road waved the bus forward and Lol could see a police Mini Metro parked at the side of the road, presumably the one which had been following them.

So Baz had been right. It had stopped to help the old man. But knowing that did not make Lol feel any better.

He walked from the bus stop carefully rehearsing what he would tell his parents, but when he glanced at his watch he realized it was exactly the same time he usually arrived home. With any luck no one would even mention the evening.

"Hello, love, had a good time?" His mother was at the kitchen table, long lengths of cloth laid out in front of her, her scissors poised in mid-air above it.

"Do you want something to eat? I've saved you some chicken for a salad."

Although he had not eaten since lunch-time he found he was not hungry at all.

"No thanks, Mum. I'm not hungry."

"You're not sickening for something are you?" She got up from her chair and put her hand on Lol's forehead.

"For heaven's sake, Mum," he pushed her hand away angrily. "I'm fine. Just because I don't want anything to eat it doesn't mean I'm dying."

"There's no need to snap at me like that." She crossed back to the table and began chopping at the material with her scissors. "You've been like a bear with a sore head. If you find your father and me so terribly irritating I suggest you go up to your room."

He began to protest but it wasn't worth it. He did want to be alone anyway. But he couldn't relax. The sound of the car hitting the old man and the sight of the ambulance haunted him. He took off his clothes and went and had a bath but that didn't make him feel any better. He climbed into bed but he couldn't read, his concentration wavered after just a few words and he turned out the light.

If only he could find out how the old man was. Perhaps he could ring the hospital. But he didn't know his name or where he had been taken and anyway, they might recognize his voice. Perhaps there might be something in the papers the next day.

A knock at the door cut through his thoughts.

"Lol?"

His father! Just what he needed. Obviously his mother had sent him up to tear a strip off him.

"Lol, are you asleep?"

Lol scarcely dared to breathe but, after a few moments, he heard his father walk across the landing and down the stairs. He curled up in bed, pulling the covers high around his head as if he could blot out the evening's memories.

He slept badly. Every time he dropped off he saw cars racing, and always the thump as the old man's body was hit by the car. Once he woke up sweating after seeing himself being marched off by two prison warders, the woman magistrate in the hydrangea hat saying darkly: "You were warned."

When his mother came in the next morning, Lol told her he was not feeling well and didn't want to go to school. This time he did not protest when she laid a cool hand on his forehead.

"You do seem to have a temperature." It was said with a mixture of concern and, he was sure, pleasure at having been proved right. "You stay in bed for now. I'm sure having a few days off school won't hurt."

"Mum." He called her back from the landing. "Can I have a look at the paper when Dad's finished with it."

She smiled indulgently. "All right love, and what about a nice cup of tea?"

He scanned the paper carefully, but could find no mention of the accident. Maybe it wasn't serious enough to go in a national newspaper, or perhaps it had happened too late to be included. Either way, it didn't ease his worried mind.

All day long he was like a cat on hot bricks. Whenever the phone rang, and twice when the doorbell sounded, he was sure it was the police.

He thought it was the end when, seconds after he heard the clink of the receiver being put in its cradle, footsteps sounded on the stairs, followed by a gentle knock. His mother came in.

He looked up at her, feeling almost glad that the moment had come at last.

"That was Mr Jackson on the phone."

Lol was surprised. "What did he want?"

"He said never mind about last night, they'll get over it and you must go on

Saturday. I didn't really understand it all. What did happen last night?"

"Oh, I had a row with one of the boys, that's all," he told her quickly.

"Not that Biffo boy, you seemed to be getting to be really good friends. Never mind, if Mr Jackson says it's all right, it must be now, mustn't it? You shouldn't let it upset you."

When she had left the room Lol sank back against the pillow. The row at the Project seemed ridiculously unimportant now.

He was dozing when he heard the sound of the paper being put through the letter box and landing with a thud on the carpet. Quickly, he nipped out of bed and tip-toed down the stairs. Rocket, ears pricked, was already sniffing the paper ready to pick it up and take it into the kitchen.

"Leave it Rocket," he whispered and the dog wagged its short tail vigorously. As he picked up the paper with one hand he reached down and patted the dog's head with the other, then, two steps at a time, he went back upstairs.

The front page was taken up with details of a huge march by trade unionists that had clogged up the whole centre of the city. He quickly flicked through the pages until his eyes were drawn to a story at the top of page seven.

"Hit and run driver hunted" ran the headline.

"Police are today hunting the driver of a green Capri which hit an elderly man in Porchester Street last night", said the first paragraph.

"The car, which had earlier been reported stolen from outside the home of its owner, was later found abandoned.

"The pedestrian, Mr Wilfred Wickens, aged 70, of Rock Estate, is today said to be comfortable in the Lady Mildmay Hospital. He has a fractured skull and broken leg."

Lol let the paper slip from his grip and it fell to the floor. He couldn't read any more. The poor old man. A fractured skull and broken leg!

He was brought his tea in bed and though it was macaroni cheese, his favourite, he could hardly touch it. When later his parents went out to visit his aunt who lived in the next street, he went down to the telephone.

It took him some time to find the telephone number for the Lady Mildmay Hospital and when he dialled it seemed to ring for ages. He was just about to give up when a sharp voice answered.

"Er, I want to find out about a patient," he explained to the woman operator.

"What ward?" said the voice.

"I don't know. He was brought in by ambulance yesterday. He'd had an accident."

"What name?"

Lol's mind raced. What name had

the papers said?

"Wickens. Mr Wilfred Wickens."

"Ah yes, here it is. Blakestone Ward. One moment."

There was a loud click followed by several minutes' silence and at first Lol thought he had been cut off. Then the phone was picked up and a woman's voice said "Blakestone Ward".

"Hello, I wanted to know how Mr Wickens is?" Lol asked.

"Are you a relative?"

"No, I'm a . . . a friend. I just wanted to know if he's all right."

"Well," she sounded a little reluctant. "I'm only really supposed to tell relatives, but it won't do any harm if I just say he's as comfortable as can be expected."

"What exactly does that mean?" Lol persisted.

"He's an old man and he has a fractured skull. It means he's not very well but he's not in any pain at the moment. Is that all right?"

"He's not going to die, is he?" Lol hardly breathed the words.

The tone in the nurse's voice changed. Now she sounded more concerned and sympathetic.

"We can never guarantee anything," she said. "Look, why don't you come in and see him, or if you tell me your name I'll let him know you phoned."

"No. Thank you. Don't bother," and quickly Lol put the phone down.

What had the nurse said? A broken leg and a fractured skull. He went upstairs feeling devastated.

The next morning he woke early after another restive night and was already downstairs, dressed for school, when his mother came down.

"Are you sure you're feeling well enough?"

"Yes, I feel fine Mum." He didn't add that lying in bed with nothing to do just made him think all the more of the accident.

Hungrily he wolfed down the cooked breakfast his mother set in front of him.

"No one could say there is anything wrong with your appetite," his father eyed him over the top of his newspaper.

"I'm off." Lol hurriedly crammed his books into his case and got his bike out of the shed. It took him twenty minutes to cycle to school and usually he enjoyed the journey. Now it gave him no pleasure at all.

Neither did the day's lessons. Twice he was told off for not paying attention, and the class had obligingly sniggered when the geography teacher said he was like an estuary — all silted up. But it filled the time and, except for a few lapses, kept the thought of the old man from his mind.

When the bell sounded for the end of the day's lessons he dawdled down to the bike sheds. There seemed nothing to hurry home for. He went part of the way with one of the boys from his form but all he could talk about was football and who would win the cup tie at the weekend. Lol didn't even know who was playing in the cup tie.

"I don't know why you never go to football, it's great," the boy said appreciatively.

"It always seems a bit pointless, just kicking a ball around," Lol told him and the boy shook his head. He was a lost cause.

He stopped at the little sweet shop just down from the school and when he came out Baz and Greg were standing smoking by his bike.

"Thought I recognized the old wheels," said Baz, flicking ash at the bike. Lol said nothing. He pushed the chocolate into his pocket before they could nick it.

"We thought we'd just remind you that silence is golden." Baz laughed at his joke. "You haven't told anyone about the other night? Our little accident?"

"Of course not," Lol snapped. "Do you think I want to get in trouble? But he's got a fractured skull. If he dies we're all for it."

"They've got to catch us first, and so long as we keep cool they won't do that." Baz confidently ground out his cigarette end.

"They've found the car," Lol told them.

" 'Course they did, stupid. We didn't exactly hide it, did we? But there's nothing to link us to the car is there? Unless someone says something."

Lol got on his bike. "I'm not going to say anything."

"Yeah, well, you'd better not."

Lol cycled off but stopped when he got to the phone box at the end of his road. Reaching in his pocket he took out the slip of paper with the telephone number of the hospital on it. Carefully he dialled, a 10p piece ready.

This time the operator was quick. It only rang once before Lol heard the telephonist.

"Good afternoon, Mildmay Hospital," said the voice, impersonal.

"Blakestone Ward please."

"One moment." Again there was a click then silence.

"Blakestone Ward."

"Hello. I wonder if you could tell me how Mr Wickens is?"

There was a moment's hesitation.

"Are you the young man who rang before?" Lol recognized the voice. It was the same nurse.

"Yes." What was the point of denying it?

"Are you a friend of Mr Wickens?"

Lol felt a prickle of fear. Why was she asking?

"Won't you tell me your name so I can tell him you . . ." she began coaxingly, but she got no farther. In a panic Lol put the phone back on the receiver. Had she told the police about the call? Had they asked her to try and find out his name?

Trembling, he went back to his bike and pushed it up the road.

When Saturday dawned, Lol knew he had no choice but to go to the Project. He couldn't risk any trouble over non-attendance. If the others still wanted to give him a hard time he would just have to keep out of their way.

His father, who was working that day, was not at breakfast when he got down.

"Dad gone?"

"No, he's in the shed. I don't know what he's up to, but his breakfast's going to get cold if he doesn't hurry up."

As she spoke, the back door opened and his father, shirt sleeves rolled up, came in.

"I knew it was there somewhere," he said, plonking a curious metal object down on the table.

"Bill!" Lol's mother's voice was sharp. "Take that filthy thing off my table!"

"Sorry, love." But instead of taking it off the table his father simply slipped the morning paper under it. The object lay there, dusty and greasy. Lol stared at it.

"What is it?"

"Call yourself a mechanic! It's a carburettor, that's what it is."

"What's it for?"

"It's a device used in petrol engines for atomising the petrol . . ." his father began in a teacherly monotone.

"No, no," Lol interrupted. "I mean why is it on the table?"

"Exactly," his mother said sharply. "That's what I'd like to know too."

"I thought perhaps you could use it, on that banger of yours."

Lol couldn't think what to say.

"Wow, thanks dad, it's fantastic! Are you sure you don't want it any more?"

"No. I took it off that old Triumph I had — remember? But I can't see me having any further use for it, so you can have it."

"Fantastic." Lol went to the kitchen drawers and took out an old plastic bag and wrapped up the carburettor.

His hopes rose as he cycled towards the Project. It wasn't a back axle but it could perhaps bridge the bitter gap that had developed between him and the others.

Biffo was standing talking to Jacko when Lol went in. Jacko smiled but Biffo seemed indifferent.

"Feeling better?" Jacko asked and Lol nodded. He'd almost forgotten about his day off school.

"What have you got there? Your lunch?" Jacko eyed the plastic bag.

"No. I thought this might be useful." He put his hand into the bag and emerged holding the carburettor.

"Where'd you get this?" Jacko asked, taking the carburettor in his hands and eyeing it expertly.

"It isn't nicked," Lol quickly protested, and Jacko's eyebrows shot up.

"I wasn't suggesting it was."

Lol blushed. "I got it from my dad. It's off an old car of his. He doesn't want it any more."

"This will be very useful. Bessie's is really on its last legs. Lol, you and Biffo take the other one off and we'll fit this later."

If looks could kill, the one Biffo flashed at Jacko would have made him a corpse instantly. But he didn't say anything. He gave a dramatic, exaggerated sigh, then walked over to Bessie and opened her bonnet.

There wasn't much conversation, and what there was was only to do with technicalities, but Lol felt that a little of the bitterness had gone out of the atmosphere. Even the lunch break wasn't the ordeal he had expected. Lol was content to sit back and listen to the boys' conversation without joining in, except for the odd word. He was in no mood for laughing and joking but he couldn't have taken it if they had continued cold-shouldering him.

"I told you they'd forget." Jacko drew him to one side as they all packed up and prepared to go. "They just needed a bit of time, that's all."

His eyes flashed across Lol's face.

"You don't seem very pleased about their change of heart."

"Yes, I am, of course," he forced a smile. "Goodnight Jacko. See you next week." And he hurried to escape Jacko's too perceptive gaze.

Chapter Six

It was dark as he walked up the lane and he could see Biffo in the shadows a few metres ahead. He was tempted to call out, run and catch him up but then he decided against it. He didn't want to risk a rebuff.

Nevertheless he was catching up on Biffo and was surprised when a beige Cortina which had been driving towards them suddenly made a sharp turn and pulled up beside Biffo. Two men got out. They were both dressed the same — grey slacks, black shoes and check jackets under large, bulging anoraks.

As they started to talk to Biffo Lol moved his bike into the road, ready to ride off.

"Just a minute, son." The taller of the two men called to him and instantly Lol knew who they were. Police. His first instinct was to flee but he didn't get the chance. The man was beside him, holding the handlebars firmly.

"We'd just like a few words with you."

"What for? I haven't done anything wrong."

"No? Right, what's your name?"

"Why d'you want to know?"

"Just answer the question."

"Hey, this is police harassment," Biffo complained. The other policeman had come to join the one holding Lol's bike and a grudging Biffo had come too. "You can't just stop us in the street."

"Look, son," the policeman's voice was more persuasive. "We just want to ask you a few questions. Now we can either do it here, or we can all take a trip down to the police station."

Lol could feel sweat prickling his brow. His hands were cold and clammy. In contrast, he thought Biffo looked cool and controlled.

"O.K. man. Hurry up, though. I've got a hot chick waiting for me."

"Right. Let's begin again. What are your names?"

"Benjamin Cox," said Biffo.

"And you?" Both policemen looked at Lol.

"Laurence Lord."

"And where have you two just come from?"

"You know damn well," Biffo said angrily. Lol was beginning to wish he'd just answer the questions. He didn't want to antagonize the policemen.

"O.K. We've just come from the Sumner House Project, down there," and Biffo jerked his thumb in the direction of the garages.

"Where were you last Wednesday night?"

"So that was it," Lol thought. "All this was about the accident."

"At the Project." Now Biffo was laughing. "Saturdays and Wednesdays we desperadoes are off the street being good boys."

The policemen ignored his jibes.

"Until what time?"

"We're there all night from whenever we get there, say four thirty to five, until nine."

"And you?" The policeman turned back to Lol.

"What?"

"Were you there, on Wednesday night?"

Lol's throat felt so dry he didn't think he would be able to speak.

" 'Course he was there," Biffo loudly interrupted. "Me and him's a team. We're the best banger boys in the business."

The policemen eyed them both carefully.

"O.K., you can go."

"Hey man, ain't you gonna tell us what all this interrogation was about?"

One of the policemen had already crossed to the driver's side of the car but the other turned back to the boys.

"An old man got run down by a hit and run. He's died. We think the car was being used by joyriders."

Lol had to clutch the frame of his bike to keep himself from falling down. His legs felt as if they were jelly.

"Pigs," Biffo shouted after the disappearing car. "Once you been in trouble they just can't leave you alone. Pigs," and he flashed a wide V-sign after the now vanished car.

"Are you all right?" his attention was caught by Lol, still weakly leaning forward over his bike. "Even in this dark you look whiter than white. You shouldn't let them get to you."

"No, you're right." Lol desperately wanted to tell Biffo what had happened but now, now that he knew the old man had died, he just couldn't.

"See you next week." He got on his bike and pedalled unsteadily off up the street.

"See you," Biffo shouted to his back.

There was a note on the kitchen table when he got in. "Gone to Aunt Edie's. Back late. Pie in oven. Mum and Dad."

Rocket was sitting in his basket, his tonque out, panting and Lol went over, crouching down beside him.

"Oh Rocket, whatever am I going to do?" He felt hot tears in his eyes and nestled down against the dog's soft silky coat. "I didn't do anything. It wasn't my fault. Oh Rocket. He's dead. He's dead," and he collapsed against the dog, sobbing noisily.

He went into the sitting-room and watched television. Or rather, the television was on and he sat in front of it. Afterwards Lol had difficulty remembering anything of what he had seen. They were just pictures flashing in front of his eyes. There was no meaning to them. Rocket lay watching him with soft, brown eyes.

He went to bed before his parents got home but he could not sleep. It was just before dawn that he finally fell into a fretful doze.

The next morning he woke feeling exactly as he had felt every morning since the crash.

At first there was a numbness, an emptiness. It was as if his brain wanted him to be cheerful but there was something, something he couldn't quite remember, preventing it.

Then the memory hit him, plunging him into an anguished awareness. And afterwards, the dread.

Downstairs his mother was busy cooking although she broke off to put some cereal in a bowl for him. By the time he had finished his chores, including braving the drizzle to take Rocket for a walk in the park, the kitchen was filled with the smell of cooking.

If his mother was surprised when he offered to help with the washing up, she didn't show it, and she rambled on happily about Auntie Edie and his cousins. He half listened, but it wasn't enough to keep his mind free from the memory of the old man.

"I'm going round to see Biffo," he suddenly announced. "We're not eating until tea are we?"

"I can make you a sandwich for your lunch if you like."

"No, it's O.K. I'll get something when I get back."

He didn't know what suddenly made him want to see Biffo, but as he cycled across town to his house he felt as if a weight had been lifted from him. He would tell Biffo. He *had* to tell someone.

As he drew up outside the block of shabby flats where Biffo lived Lol could hear music blaring out. The rain had long stopped and several people were sitting on the wall outside the flats, enjoying the thin sunshine and chatting.

He didn't want to leave his bike outside. Biffo had told him that things had a habit of "walking" if you weren't careful, so he hauled it up a flight of steep concrete steps into the hallway. Then he chained it to the stair bannister. The music got louder with every step he climbed. He could just imagine how his parents would react to reggae full blast on a Sunday.

He knocked on the purple-painted door and it was opened almost immediately by a large, fat woman obviously dressed in her Sunday best.

"Hello, Mrs Cox. Is Biffo in?"

"Hello, Lol, come on in." She went back into the room, searching for something amongst the jumble of clothes on the settee. "Biffo? No, I'm sorry, Lol, he's gone over to see his sister. She's just moved into her new flat." Triumphantly she uncovered what she was looking for, a white glove.

"He should be back by about half past seven. You come round then if you like. Have some dinner." With Lol preceding her she went out of the flat and locked the door behind her.

"Thanks, Mrs Cox. But I think my mum's made me some dinner. Maybe I'll see Biffo later, anyway."

"You do that, Lol. Now you've got to excuse me, I'm late for chapel." And she hurried across the hallway to greet a friend coming out of another flat.

Lol cycled around aimlessly. Since joining the Project he seemed to have lost touch with all his old friends. All they were interested in was football or girls. He knew that several boys from his class would probably be down at the playing fields but he couldn't be bothered to join them.

So he went home. His father was working so he and his mother ate their tea on their laps in front of the television.

"If your dad keeps up with all this

overtime I think we could afford a holiday," she told Lol. "He's already mentioned it."

"The Lake District?" That was where his parents always went when they could afford a holiday. In fact that, and one week in Devon, was the only place Lol had been to outside London.

"No. Spain, your father thought, though don't you dare tell him I mentioned it. I think he wants it to be a surprise."

"Spain!" It had never occurred to Lol that they might actually go abroad. Just wait until he told the others.

Lol made no secret of the fact that he did not like school but of all the days Mondays were the most tolerable. He had two free periods in the morning and, in the afternoon, athletics. He was good at athletics and it was the one subject where he didn't seem to be continually in trouble.

He had played hookey too often to be really top class, but when he put his mind to it he found he could always come at least second, and often first. It gave him a buzz. Not only the winning but the hard physical exertion.

"You know, Lord," the athletics coach held him back when the session was ended, "if you'd only put in a bit of time training you could be good, really good. I hate to see talent going to waste. Why don't you come along to Athletics Club on Wednesdays?"

Lol's heart fell. He had been just about to jump at the chance but he couldn't — not on Wednesdays, Project night — but he wasn't going to admit that to the coach.

"Sorry, Mr Briggs," he said, feigning indifference. "I just like running for fun. I don't fancy racing round and round a track all the time."

"It's your loss, boy."

If Lol had been more alert he would have seen the car before he walked into his home, but his mind was still on the athletics. So the first thing he knew about the visitors was when he heard voices in the sitting room and his father called him in.

The second he stepped through the door Lol recognized the two men now sitting slightly self-consciously in the armchairs. It was the two policemen who had stopped him and Biffo earlier.

"Laurence, these two men are policemen. They want to ask you a few questions." His father stood with one hand protectively on Lol's shoulders.

"Yes." Lol looked uneasily at the two men.

"It's about that acci . . ." his father began.

"If you don't mind, Mr Lord, I think I'd rather ask the questions," the tall policeman interrupted.

"Very well, officer." It was said reluctantly.

"Do you know Basil Davids and Gregory Church?"

There was no point denying it. Everyone, including the police, knew about him and Baz.

"Yes. Why?"

"Are you friends?"

"I know them. We were friends."

"Were? Aren't you any more?"

"I haven't seen them for ages."

"That's right, officer. We told him to stay away from them and he has done," his father told them.

"Thank you, sir." The policeman acknowledged Lol's dad, then turned his attention back to Lol.

"Exactly when did you last see them?"

Lol was silent.

"Roughly," the policeman prompted. Again Lol was silent.

"Why do you need to know all this? Laurence hasn't done anything wrong. Why aren't you questioning the other two boys if you are so interested in them?" His father was beginning to get angry, his face red.

"We have talked to them, sir," it was the other policeman who now talked. "And they indicated that Laurence might be able to help us further."

"I didn't do it, it wasn't me." The words spilled out before Lol could think.

"What didn't you do, son?"

Lol dropped his head down.

"I think you'd better come down to the

station with us." And before his father could protest again, he added. "You may come too if you wish, sir."

"Oh, Laurence," his mother spoke for the first time. "What's it all about? Tell them you haven't been up to anything."

"I think it would be better if we sorted this out at the station, madam." The big policeman began to walk towards the front door. His father, who had gone out to get his jacket, was already standing there.

"Wait for me, I'll get my coat," his mother began stripping off her apron.

"No, love, you stay here. We'll be back in no time, I'm sure."

When they got to the car, the same beige Cortina, the taller policeman got inside and leaned across to open the passenger door for the other man. As he leaned back to open the rear door, Lol saw his chance. It wasn't thought out or planned. It was purely instinctive. He saw his chance and took it. He gave the front door a slight shove that sent the policeman tumbling back into the foot-well and then raced off down the street, head down, arms pumping, forcing his legs to go faster.

"Lol!" He could hear his father's cry as well as the more angry shouts of the policeman.

Lol ran blindly at first, just intent on getting away. Behind him he could vaguely hear the sound of a car engine revving. Obviously the police car. He couldn't stick to the road, he thought, he'd be caught in no time.

He veered off, hauling himself over the fence into the grounds of the primary school. He tore across the playground and went round the back of the building.

He skidded to a halt as he found himself face to face with a huge brick wall. Frantically he looked round for something to climb on. He pulled the dustbins towards the wall, wincing at the loud scraping noise they made, then stood on one and pulled himself up onto the top of the wall, balancing there for a few seconds before dropping down the other side.

He was just inside. On the other side of the wall he could hear the sound of running footsteps.

It was rough ground and several times he stumbled, but eventually he arrived at the main road again. There was no sign of the police car and, looking behind him, he could see nothing of the policeman who had been chasing him.

But Lol didn't feel safe, and though he didn't know where to go he set off running.

Children stopped to watch as he raced through the play ground, and he almost knocked an old man off his feet when he crashed through the park entrance.

"Oi, young man, you just watch where you're going!" the old chap's voice sounded angry but shaky and brought back a flash memory of the old man lying in the road.

When he got to the main road he was frantic. He couldn't run much more, his breath was coming in deep gasps that burned his throat, and his side ached.

He saw the sign first — "God, your refuge" — in huge yellow letters on a big ornate blue board outside a church. Quickly, without really thinking what he was going to do, he went up to the large wooden doors. He took hold of the huge iron handle in his hands. At first nothing happened, then, with irritating slowness, they creaked open. He only needed a small gap, then he could slide inside, shutting the doors behind him, leaning against them, panting.

It had been years since he was last in church. When he was little he used to go to church with the school, but neither of his parents were churchgoers so when he had moved up to the senior school he had just got out of the habit.

He walked up the side aisle, his running shoes making a quiet squishing sound on the parquet floor. It was an old church, dark and cold. Everywhere there were statues or pictures. On the altar, one large candle burned dimly.

As Lol sat on one of the wood pews he felt more than a little ridiculous. It was like a scene from a bad movie. The escaped convict hiding out in the church.

Could he ask for sanctuary? Lol wasn't sure of the law now, but he had a feeling that too only happened in the films. Anyway, who wanted to spend the rest of their lives in a church?

Finally, when his bottom was aching from sitting on the hard wood seat and he was bored with nothing to read or look at, he decided to chance his luck outside again.

Cautiously he poked his head around the church door. It was cold and almost dark and the rain had started again but there was no sign of the police. He pulled his anorak tightly about him, putting up the collar before stuffing his hands into his pocket.

His first thought was to go round to Biffo's house but he quickly dismissed the idea — that would probably be the first place the police would go.

He felt in his pocket and his fingers touched some coins. He drew out his hand eagerly and looked down at the open palm. There was a 50p, two 10ps, a 5p and six pennies. He wasn't going to get far on that.

A few minutes later some of it had gone and he munched his way through a large bag of chips. He had wanted the fish as well but he felt he should keep some money for emergencies.

When he had finished, he scrunched the paper up into a tight ball, which he lobbed neatly into a nearby rubbish bin.

The door of a telephone kiosk beside him swung open and a woman came out. Lol watched her walk away then fished in his pocket and got out another tenpenny piece. He put it in the money slot, ready, then dialled.

"Hello? Hello?" his mother's voice sounded briefly, then almost immediately he heard the pips. It was stiff and at first he thought he wasn't going to be able to make it work but eventually he managed to push the coin in. There was a clicking sound, then he heard her voice again.

"Hello?" she repeated.

"Mum!"

"Laurence, is that you?" Relief flooded into her voice.

"Yes, Mum." His voice was breaking with emotion and he felt close to tears.

"Where are you?" But before he had time to answer he heard his father's voice.

"Laurence, where on earth are you?"

"I'm all right, Dad," Lol told him.

"What the hell are you doing, running away? It won't solve anything, it'll only make things worse. You've got to come back and face them. We'll stand by you, son."

"But they won't believe me, Dad. The old man died. I couldn't stand being locked away, I just couldn't."

"I know, son, but you can't just run off, your mother's frantic with worry."

"I'm sorry, Dad but . . ." The conversation was broken by a series of loud pips. Frantically Lol searched in his pocket, but he couldn't find the coins. After a few minutes the pips ended and there was a long shrill tone. They'd been cut off.

Lol set off walking towards the Project. He knew there was nowhere else for him to go. Mondays and Tuesdays Jacko went to teach evening sessions at the College of Further Education so he knew he wouldn't be around. It would give him time to think and plan what he was going to do next.

It took Lol twice as long to get there as usual because he deliberately kept off the main roads in case the police were still looking for him. When he arrived, the lane down to the Project was eerily quiet. The dim light from the few street lamps cast grey puddles of light. A car, reversing out of the drive of one of the houses, made Lol sink back against the hedge but the driver passed without noticing him at all.

Pausing at the gates he carefully studied the house. There were no lights upstairs and just one in the downstairs front room. Silently he ran towards the garage. Once there was the sound of barking inside the house but then someone shouted and the dog was silent.

Although the main doors were kept locked he knew that with a bit of gentle "persuasion" he could open the little side window beside the back door.

It was easier than he had expected. Balancing on an old oil drum, he gave it a jab with the heel of his hand and it swung open. He waited, listening, but there was no sound and with a little hop he pulled himself up on to the window sill then swung his legs inside and dropped to the floor.

Inside he could see very little. There was a deep, pungent smell of oil and petrol but at least it was slightly warmer than outside.

Cautiously, arms out in front of him like a blind man, he made his way to the work bench. It took some time. It was difficult rummaging around in the dark, particularly as he had to be careful not to knock anything over in case someone heard the noise, but eventually he found what he was looking for — the torch.

The light wasn't very bright but that was probably to his advantage. At least it was unlikely to be spotted from outside.

He scanned the bench but there was nothing of any interest, just a few dirty rags. He swung the torch upwards and stopped when he found a half-empty packet of biscuits. He reached up and grabbed them, hungrily devouring two in one go. Despite the chips he had eaten earlier, he was still hungry.

Under the bench he found a carton of milk but when he sniffed it, it was sour and made his stomach heave. Finally he settled for a swig of metallic-tasting water from the spout of the kettle. There wasn't much but it was better than nothing.

He shone the torch at his watch. It said six-thirty . . . but it couldn't be. Lol shook it then held it to his ear. "Damn," he thought, "it's stopped." He had no idea what time it was. The events of the evening had merged into minutes or hours, he wasn't sure which.

He looked around the garage for somewhere to sit down, but apart from a few oil drums and some old wheels, there was nothing. He leaned back against Bessie, cold and unyielding in the dark, and realized he had found the perfect place.

The back door was stiff but he eventually managed to get it open. He clambered in, pulling it close behind him. Despite her great age and previous ill-treatment at who knew how many hands, the back seat was surprisingly comfortable. A little lumpy, and there was a rip in the front which leaked prickly horsehair that he could feel as he searched for something he could pull over himself. The tarpaulin stuffed down in the footwell was old and rather smelly, but after he had got used to the initial dampness, felt quite warm.

Chapter Seven

Lol had not expected to sleep, but with a welcome blankness, he did. When he woke it was as if he was dreaming. None of the surroundings looked familiar, even the smell was strange, but then the memory of the previous day flooded his mind.

Judging by the light that filtered through the window, thin and watery, it was quite early. He looked at his watch, then irritated, remembered it was not working.

He was just about to emerge from his hiding place when the sound of a key in the lock sent him cringing back under the green cover, trying to press his body farther into Bessie's slightly unyielding seats.

The trouble was that being so low down he could not see what was going on and had to rely on what he could hear.

There was a bang as the door swung open and light flooded the garage. There was the sound of footsteps, a creaking, and the light faded again. Whoever it was had pulled the door shut behind them. At first he thought they had gone away but he heard more footsteps, and the sound of tools being moved about on the bench.

"Hello, Bessie, and how are you this morning?" The sudden sound of a voice, quite loud, made him jump. Then he relaxed a little, it was instantly recognizable as Gill. Lol had to smile to himself. Only Gill would have a conversation with a car!

"I thought I'd give you a little beauty treatment — how do you fancy that?"

The mind boggled. What on earth was she talking about, Lol wondered. Beauty treatment?

He heard a tap running and the sound of metal scraping against metal. Of course, she was filling the kettle. Just the thought of a cup of tea made his mouth water.

There was more clanking about then another creak and light swamped the room again. "She's going out" Lol thought. He decided now was his chance to get away. Whatever she was up to she was likely to discover him sooner or later. As soon as the door clicked shut he threw off the tarpaulin and sat upright. He'd have to be quick, he didn't know how long she would be gone.

When he tried to move he let out a little yelp. His whole leg was numb where it had been curled up. He leaned down and rubbed it briskly then forced it out straight. Whoever said pins and needles was a pleasant sensation must be mad he thought. As the blood surged back into the cramped muscles, it felt as if he were literally being touched by hundreds of red hot pins.

He pressed down on the door handle and pushed at the door with his shoulder but it wouldn't budge. He tried again. Finally he wound down the window. He'd have to get out that way.

Lol had just got the top half of his body out and was sitting on the edge of the window when he heard the door opening. The widening shaft of light cut across him before he could drop back down into the car.

"What on earth?" Gill's exclamation was horribly loud.

"*Shush*," he hissed sharply at her.

"Lol?" Now he could see her surprised face, her eyes wide in disbelief. "What are you doing here?"

"*Shush*, Gill, keep your voice down! Someone will hear."

She glanced over her shoulder then drew the garage door shut behind her.

"O.K?" Now her voice was scarcely more than a whisper. "Now tell me what on earth you're doing here. Have you been here all night?"

"Is your father coming out here this morning?" he asked, as this time he successfully managed to get out of Bessie's window.

"Dad? He might do, I don't know. Do you want to talk to him?"

"*No!*" The shout was loud and determined and surprised her. "No," Lol repeated more softly.

"What's up, are those guys who beat you up after you?"

He wondered if he could somehow avoid telling her, but he realized that he was in her hands. He had to trust her.

"The police are after me."

"The police! But why?"

Again he hesitated but he reckoned she'd know soon enough anyway. The police were bound to call and see Jacko.

"You know that old man that got run down?"

"Which old man?"

"An old man who was knocked down while he was crossing a road down on the industrial estate."

"But what's that got to do with you?"

"If you'd stop interrupting I'd tell you. I was in the car."

"Oh, Lol!" She sounded shocked.

"I wasn't driving," his voice appealed. "I was in the back, but I know the police won't believe me."

"But who *was* driving? Why don't you

just tell the police?"

"I can't. Oh Gill, can't you see that I can't. Anyway, even if I did it would be their word against mine. No one would believe me."

"What are you going to do?"

"I thought I could hide out here at least until tomorrow."

"But then what?"

"I don't know, I'll think of something."

"Lol, you can't just keep running. Why don't you give yourself up? Dad would help you, I'm sure."

"I can't, Gill, I can't. They'd send me away this time. Detention centre. I couldn't stand that. You won't tell anyone will you — not even your dad."

She considered for a few moments then, with a sigh, agreed.

"Have you had anything to eat?"

"Not really. I found some biscuits last night but . . ."

"Right. You stay here and I'll go and find you something. You'd better hide, just in case, until I get back."

He nodded and she turned to go.

"Gill," he felt a rising panic as she walked towards the door. "Promise you won't say anything?"

"Oh sure," she said in an offhand way. "I just thought I'd nip off and ring the CID while your egg and bacon is cooking."

After she had gone, he obediently got back in Bessie and pulled the tarpaulin over his head. At the sound of the door opening again his inside fluttered but then he heard her voice calling out and folded back the tarpaulin.

"Here you are," she said, leaning through the car's open window. "Breakfast," and she handed over a huge doorstep sandwich dripping with jam.

"Thanks!" He grabbed the sandwich and ate ravenously, crumbs falling from his mouth, a tiny drip of jam falling on to his jumper. She didn't speak until he had finished.

"More?" She held out a banana.

"Thanks." But he didn't eat it. He pushed it into his pocket, anticipating a long gap between meals.

"I've brought you a book. I thought you might get a bit bored all alone in here."

"Great," but his enthusiasm faded when he read the title, *Lord of the Flies*. They had been told to read that during the last holiday but he had never got past the first few pages. Books didn't interest him much.

She looked at her watch. "I've got to go now, my mum wants me to help her. I'll come back when I can."

When she had gone Lol felt terribly alone. Whatever the books or TV made out, being wanted by the police was no lark. After lying still, thinking, for some time, he opened the book and idly glanced at the lines of small type. But gradually he became absorbed as the story of the boys' fight for survival, and supremacy, unfolded. He was so engrossed he didn't hear the footsteps approaching and he leapt as if scalded when the lock rattled noisily and the door was flung open.

"Lol, the police are here." Gill's voice was high pitched and frantic. But now that it had happened Lol felt strangely calm.

"Where are they?"

"In the house, talking to Dad."

"What did they say?"

"There's only one, in plain clothes."

"O.K., what did *he* say?"

"He said that you'd done a bunk and did Dad have any idea where you were?"

"What did your dad say?"

"I don't know. I got out of the house as quick as I could so I could warn you. What are you going to do?"

"Get out of here." He squeezed out through the open window.

"But he'll see you."

"Not if I go this way," and he crossed to the small window he had used to get in. "Look, I'll duck down until he's gone. If it's all clear call out of the window, otherwise try to buy me enough time to get away."

"How?"

"I don't know. Think of something," he said before disappearing out of the small window.

He was just in time. As he went out there was the sound of voices outside. Gill hurriedly closed the little window, picked up a spanner from the bench, and pulled on an overall.

When the garage door opened and two figures walked in she was head down over the radiator, apparently struggling with a rusty jubilee clip that was fastened to a perished rubber hose.

"There you are."

Gill raised her head at her father's voice and smiled at him.

"How's it going?" He sounded quite calm and natural.

"Fine. I'm just taking off the old hose so I can put the new one on."

"I thought you were giving your mother a hand."

"Oh, Dad, you know I hate the washing up. I'll be finished soon."

"I don't know, what would you do with her?" Jacko turned to the policeman. "Other men's daughters love helping round the house, cooking meals and all that. Mine takes delight in stripping down engines."

The policeman laughed. Slowly he paced the garage, picking up a spanner, moving a rag, generally nosing around. Then he leaned inside the open window on Bessie's back door. Gill held her breath but he straightened up and, without further comment, continued his prowling.

"Have you seen Laurence Lord recently?" he asked Gill.

"Who?" She was genuinely puzzled.

"Laurence Lord," the policeman repeated.

"Lol," her father explained, and she mouthed a silent "Oh". "He's missing."

"Missing?" she repeated.

"When did you last see him?" The policeman stared at Gill, his full attention on her face.

"Saturday." She didn't hesitate. "With the others."

"You haven't seen him since?"

"No." She held the policeman's stare until he eventually turned away.

"Right, Mr Jackson. Thank you. I'm sorry I had to bother you. And thank you too, Miss Jackson." The two men walked from the garage and Gill heard them talking outside. Then there was the sound of footsteps walking towards the lane, making a scrunching sound on the rough surface.

Gill waited until the sound had faded before opening the garage door and looking out. Her father was just climbing into his car and, with a jaunty wave to her, he too was gone.

"All clear," she called softly out of the small window. Two hands appeared on the sill, then, with a hop, Lol pulled himself inside.

"What happened?" He was panting slightly from the effort.

"Nothing much. He just had a snoop around and asked when I'd last seen you. I didn't know your real name was

Laurence," she grinned.

"What did you tell him?" Lol ignored the jibe.

"Last Saturday, what else?"

He looked at her, taking in for the first time that she was in school uniform. If he was playing hookey so must she be.

"How come you're not at school?"

"Dentist. I've got an appointment at eleven. Mum went mad because I made it in school time, but as we had to cancel the last one she couldn't cancel this too. Clever, eh?"

"Yes, I suppose so." He wasn't really listening. "What time is it?"

She glanced at her watch. "Quarter past ten."

Silently he corrected his watch and wound it up.

"Could you do me a favour?"

"Sure." She was eager, eyes bright with excitement.

"Get a message to Biffo. Tell him what's happened. Ask him if he can come here."

"I thought you two weren't speaking."

She had a point there but Lol thought — hoped — that perhaps if he knew he was in trouble Biffo might forget their old quarrel.

"Just say I need his help."

"Anything else?"

"Tell him to be careful. I don't want him to get in any trouble too."

"O.K. Will he be at home?"

"He should be — he left school last term. If not, he'll probably be down the Tempo."

"The café?"

"Yeah. He knows the guy who owns it. I think he helps out sometimes. Earns a bit of money on the side."

"What time shall I tell him to come?"

"Whenever he can. It doesn't matter, I'm not going anywhere," he added bitterly.

"I've got to go to school after the dentist but I'll see you this evening. I'll try and bring you some more food. See you." She shut the door behind her and once again he heard the turn of the key in the padlock. It made him feel strangely safe.

He considered doing some work on Bessie, it would help fill in the time, but he was afraid that Mrs Jackson might hear. So instead he climbed back inside Bessie and curled up on the back seat, soon losing himself in the tale of the island castaways.

"*Pssst.*"

Lol looked up. He could see nothing, hear nothing, and decided he must have imagined the sound.

"*Psst* Lol." He definitely heard it that time. Cautiously he raised his head above the back of Bessie's seat but still he could see nothing.

"For gawd's sake man, open the window." He heard that all right. He leapt up and crossed to the small window which was open a crack but still on the catch. He looked down onto the gleaming tombstone smile of Biffo.

"About bloomin' time too, man," he moaned, as he hauled himself through the window and dropped nimbly down on to the garage floor.

They stared at each other in easy silence. Lol was relieved that all the friction of their last few meetings seemed to have vanished.

"This is one hell of a mess you're in," he said.

"You're telling me," Lol replied with feeling.

"What's going down exactly?"

"Didn't Gill tell you?"

"Not really. She came bursting in the café just as I was getting on re-al good with a girl I've been hankering after for a long time, drags me away and says I've got to come and see you, that you're in trouble. My girl — I don't think she understood one bit when I upped and left her."

Lol could just imagine the scene.

"Thanks for coming anyway, Biffo," and he began to outline what had happened.

"Man, what a load of trouble. Who was driving?"

Again Lol hesitated, this time as much from embarrassment as anything else. He knew what Biffo's reaction would be.

"Baz," he finally admitted.

"Baz! And you're surprised you're in trouble. Haven't you got any sense! Was the car stolen?"

"Yes — but I didn't know that at the beginning. He said he'd borrowed it."

"And you believed him?"

It did sound pretty weak.

"Why did you go with him at all?" Biffo wanted to know.

"I was mad with you lot, you'd been giving me a hard time since the smash. I didn't really think."

"Well we'd better do some thinking now. How much do the police know?"

"I'm not sure. They just said that Baz and Greg had told them I might be able to help them."

Biffo considered. "They can't be sure they were driving or they'd have hauled them in. Were they wearing gloves?" Lol couldn't remember.

"Were you?" Biffo knew the answer from Lol's face.

They were both silent for a while, thinking.

"Seems to be you've got two alternatives," Biffo said finally. "Either you go to the police and give yourself up . . ."

"I can't do that. No one would believe me, you know they won't. They'll think it was me. They haven't got anything on Baz and Greg."

". . . Or," Biffo ignored the outburst.

"Or we find some way to make Baz and Greg confess."

Lol looked at him as if he had finally gone off his nut.

"And how the hell do we do that," he shouted. "Excuse me, Baz and Greg," he feigned a soft, upper-class accent, "do you think you could be so kind as to go to the police and admit you were driving the car and that our friend Laurence here was a mere innocent bystander. You're mad!"

"No, we've got to persuade them."

"Persuade them! How, for heaven's sake? They're like bloomin' tanks. They'd make mincemeat of us."

"True. But there's only two of them."

"And there's only two of us."

"No," Biffo corrected him. "There's ten of us."

"Ten?"

"Sure. You, me, Alan. Zac . . ." He began counting off names on his fingers.

"We can't involve them. I feel bad enough about you and Gill knowing."

"Look man, we stick together," Biffo's face was serious. "Bessie's Banger Boys, that's what the sign says. No one's got any love for Baz and Greg. I reckon they must have done the dirty to just about everyone. They'll only get what they deserve."

"But how will you do it?"

"You leave that to me. I'll let you know." He stood up, brushing down his trousers. "Right, now I'm getting back to my girl. You O.K. here for a while?"

"I guess so. Gill says Jacko's away for the day."

"Right. I'll be back later." And he climbed onto the bench and disappeared through the window.

Gill reappeared first. Lol heard footsteps but then her voice called out. "It's only me" as she unlocked the door. She was still wearing her school uniform but out of her coat pocket she produced two packets of crisps, a Kit Kat, an apple and a small carton of orange juice. Lol fell on the feast ravenously. The banana and the rest of the biscuits had gone at lunchtime and now his stomach was graunching with hunger.

Lol ate while Gill recounted what had happened to her at the dentist and her version of the scene at the café. Lol was worried that her presence in the garage might make her mother suspicious, but she assured him that her mother never noticed what she got up to, and Jacko wouldn't be back until much later.

At the sound of a light tap on the little window Gill climbed up and pushed it open. Seconds later Biffo appeared and dropped down to the floor. Following him was another, older boy whom Lol didn't recognize.

"This is my brother-in-law, Luther," Biffo introduced them, "though most people call him Lucky." Lol nodded though he was puzzled about why Biffo had brought him at all. Didn't enough people know about him already?

As if reading his mind, Biffo went on; "He's got his van outside. We need the wheels, man, and he's the only one allowed to drive — legit like."

"His van! What for?"

"I'll explain everything later. The thing is you're going to have a visit this evening."

"A visit. Who from?" Lol had the feeling that events were rolling along affecting him but he had absolutely no control over them.

"Now that's the big surprise." Biffo was obviously enjoying every moment, particularly Lol's puzzled expression. "You sit tight here and we'll be back inside . . ." he consulted his watch ". . . an hour."

Lol could only agree. He'd come this far.

"You know what you got to do?" Biffo asked Gill and she nodded.

"Of course."

"O.K. No foul-ups." Then he and his brother went back out through the window and Lol heard the sound of a distant engine starting up then driving away.

"What the hell is going on? Why won't anybody let me in on the big secret?" he asked Gill angrily.

"There's a good reason, and you'll find out soon enough anyway. Why don't you finish your book? I'll be back soon."

Lol felt little prickles of apprehension rippling through his body. Although Biffo and the others were his friends, he would have felt better if he knew what they were going to do.

Time ticked by slowly. He couldn't get interested in his book again. He was too twitchy. Several times he was sure he could hear someone approaching but the garage doors remained firmly closed.

Finally he did hear something. The sound of a car engine, and it was coming to the doors. Frantically he ducked back inside Bessie, pulling the tarpaulin over him again. The engine idled and he heard the sound of voices, then the garage doors opened.

"I don't see anybody. Is this a joke?"

Lol recognized the voice. It was Baz, slightly truculent, but with an edge of fear.

"If this is a joke, you lot'll be pretty sorry."

"It's no joke," Lol heard Biffo tell him and there was the sound of several feet scuffling on the floor.

"O.K. Lol, you can come out now. It's safe," Biffo called out.

Lol threw off the tarpaulin and pushed himself up. It was an amazing sight. The garage was full of Bessie's gang and there in the centre, looking more than a little apprehensive, was Baz. His coat was muddy and there was a graze on his cheek.

Obviously he had been a none-too-willing visitor.

He enjoyed the surprised expression on Baz's face as he climbed out of Bessie though he quickly covered it up.

"Hey, Lol." Baz became nauseatingly friendly. "What's all this about? Sending your friends down to kidnap me. You should have just asked, I'd have come."

"Kidnap!" scoffed Biffo. "Man, we just asked you — real polite — to come and have a quick chat and we provided the transport. Is it our fault if you're clumsy and fall over your own feet?"

Baz scowled at him but obviously felt intimidated by the presence of the other boys and did nothing.

"I wanted to have a few words," Lol explained. "And as, thanks to you, the police are after me, I thought you might be kind enough to come here."

"A few words about what?"

"You know damn well. About the hit and run."

"Hit and run. What hit and run?" His face was an exaggerated picture of innocence.

"You told them it was me."

"Don't be so daft. I just said I thought I'd seen someone who looked a bit like you driving a car. It was a joke."

"A joke!" Biffo took a step towards Baz, fist raised. "That's a very peculiar sense of humour you've got."

"They're trying to pin it on me," Lol

continued, sounding a lot calmer than he felt.

"Pin what?" Baz had returned to his role of local dimwit.

Lol sighed. He was getting nowhere.

"Come on, Baz, you know perfectly well that I wasn't driving that car."

There was silence but the boys were beginning to grow restless. Baz eyed them cautiously.

"I'll tell you what," Baz put his arm around Lol's shoulders. "You get rid of your minders and we'll have a little chat. How about that?"

Lol glanced at the faces standing in a semi-circle in front of him. He knew he wouldn't get anywhere until they had gone.

"O.K.," he agreed. "Biffo. Can you and the lads wait outside? Just for a few minutes?"

Biffo looked suspiciously at Baz.

"You'd better not cause no trouble man," he gave him a sharp poke in the chest, "Or we'll be back in here like lightning."

"All right. Watch the jacket," Baz brushed Biffo's hands from his coat front. He was beginning to regain much of his usual confidence. Slowly, with menacing backward glances, the boys filed outside and closed the garage door behind them.

"Now that's more sensible," Baz said, pulling himself up so he was sitting on Bessie's front wing.

"Look, Baz," Lol stood in front of him. "That old bloke died. You're trying to pin it on me."

"Stupid old geezer," Baz's voice was vicious. "He shouldn't have stepped out."

"They'll lock me away if they catch me."

"Well, ain't that a shame!"

"You know I wasn't driving."

"And what do you suggest I do? Go down to the police station and say; 'Hey Mr Policeman, don't send Lol to prison, I was the one driving. Send me instead.' You must be off your trolley."

"But it isn't fair."

"Look, kid. O.K. so it's tough, but I'm not going to drop myself in it just to get you off the hook. You'll have to find your own way out of this."

"I'll tell the police then," Lol told him.

"You do that," Baz sounded triumphant. "Who's going to believe your word against me and Greg? No one knows we was in the car, they can't prove anything. We had gloves on, we ain't stupid. It's just your luck for being in the wrong place at the wrong time."

"But you admitted you were driving, just now."

"Look, you know I was driving and I know I was driving but no one else does. Who heard? Your mates outside? No way. I'll just deny I ever said anything. No one will believe you."

"I will."

The voice made both boys jump. Lol looked round and saw the bearded figure of Jacko emerging from behind the door that linked the two garages, and behind him, grinning broadly, was Gill.

Baz turned and looked frantically around the garage for some means of escape. He made a rush for the doors but at that moment they opened and Biffo, Alan and the rest of the gang stood there.

"I've been set up," Baz snarled angrily whirling round and, before anyone could stop him, lashing out wildly at Lol.

It all happened so quickly, it wasn't until afterwards that Lol really felt the pain. He just felt an incredible thud and then found himself on the floor.

"As you all right?" Gill was instantly at his side, but when he once again became aware of where he was, Lol was more interested in the melee involving Baz and several of the boys.

"Come on, knock it off, knock it off." Jacko waded in, pulling several boys off before picking up Biffo with one firm hand, Baz with the other. They were still locked in an angry embrace. Eventually, punches flying in the air, Biffo was held back.

"You set yourself up when you decided to let Lol carry the can," Jacko told Baz.

"Now, may I suggest that we all take a little drive down to the police station."

Gleefully, the boys ushered Baz out of the garage. Joseph and Alan, having been judged the strongest, were given the job of guards and they each firmly held one of Baz's arms.

"What will happen to me?" Lol asked Jacko, still trembling slightly from the punch.

"That's up to the police. It was stupid to run off and you've put everyone to an awful lot of trouble."

Lol sighed. "Will they believe me now?"

"I think so. You've got a lot to thank the others for, you know."

"Yes, I do," and he realized that he had not in fact thanked Biffo or any of them. "How did you find out what was going on?"

"Gill rang me at the college. She didn't tell me what was going on, she just said it was very important and I was to leave my car in the lane — obviously that was so you wouldn't hear it, get worried, and take off."

"I didn't know you were there," Lol conceded.

"No, I know. The others thought you might give the game away. Ask too obvious questions. They had a good point but I can't say I approve of acting outside the law. Still, in this case it looks as if it has paid off."

It was quite a convoy that travelled to the police station. Jacko and Lol were in the front of the Cortina with Baz sandwiched in between Joseph and Alan in the back. Following them was Lucky's van containing all the rest.

"What about my parents?" Lol suddenly remembered them.

"We'll call them from the police station. They'll be so relieved. They've been out of their minds with worry."

When they turned into the police station Lol felt a sinking feeling in his gut. Suppose, after all this, the police still didn't believe him? But now that he had got this far there was no alternative.

Baz struggled weakly when they got out of the car, but his two guards were standing no nonsense and eventually he "allowed" himself to be helped up the steps.

"Good evening." Jacko leaned on the desk talking to a uniformed sergeant.

"Good evening Mr Jackson." He eyed the curious band of boys now filling the entrance hall. "What can I do for you?"

"Is Det Sgt Henderson in?"

"I think you may just have caught him sir, one moment," and he turned away, picking up a telephone and speaking quietly into the receiver. Then he replaced it and turned back to Jacko.

"He's on his way, Sir." Then, catching sight of Baz, still held tight by Joseph and Alan, he added, "Can I be of any assistance."

"No, it's all right, thank you. I think my young friends have everything under control."

The sergeant nodded agreement.

Suddenly, with a bang, the solid wood door beside the front desk burst open and the policeman who had called at Lol's house and who had later come to the garage came in.

"Hello, Mr Jackson, and what have you got for me here?" He too eyed the group, his eyes resting longer on Lol and Baz.

"I see you've found my runaway."

"Ah yes, well, I would like a little word with you if I may, Sgt Henderson. But perhaps you could put this young man" — he indicated Baz — "somewhere safe first so the rest of the lads can go home?"

"Sergeant," Sgt Henderson turned to the uniformed sergeant. "Could you find some nice cosy little room where that young gentleman may sit while I have a brief conversation with Mr Jackson."

Another phone call, and a lanky young policeman appeared and led Baz away.

"Right, this way Mr Jackson. Let's go and have that little chat shall we?" Sgt Henderson held out his arm in the direction of the door.

"O.K. lads," Jacko turned back to the boys. "Thanks for all your help. I'll talk to you all tomorrow." Then he and Lol preceded the detective through the door.

Lol was shown into a small room painted a dull green and cream and told to sit on one of the two chairs beside a table.

"Wait there. I won't be a minute," the

detective told him. "Meanwhile this nice young policewoman will keep you company."

Lol stared at the door for several moments after it had clanked shut. He caught the eye of the young policewoman but she remained, unsmiling, at attention. The only light in the room came from a fluorescent light strip that flickered and made a curious fizzing sound. The only window was high up, and covered with two sturdy-looking metal bars.

Finally he leaned back in the chair, staring blankly at the empty table, watching and listening as the second hand on the clock moved slowly round.

Automatically he stood up straight when the door swung open. Sgt Henderson and Jacko came back in.

"Another chair, please," the detective asked the policewoman, putting down the cup he was carrying. After a brief pause she returned with another chair identical to the others. She gave it to Jacko who, moving it slightly away from the table, sat down.

Sgt Henderson walked slowly over to the other chair, still pushed in at the table and stood, leaning on it, watching Lol. He picked up the spoon, stirred the tea vigorously, put the spoon in the saucer, and drank. Then he put the cup back on the table.

"Do you know how much trouble you've

caused everyone by this little jaunt of yours?" he said finally, drawing the chair out and sprawling on it. Lol didn't answer.

"Nothing to say for yourself?"

"I'm . . . I'm sorry," Lol eventually stammered.

"You're sorry. Oh good, that makes me feel a lot better. I have had to work overtime virtually every evening; I've had the Super breathing fire at me; the press have been having a go at police incompetence, and you tell me you're sorry. Thank you very much."

Lol bristled at the attack, but just when he was about to answer the tirade he caught Jacko's eye and saw the slight shake of his head. He remained silent.

"Now, suppose you tell me all about it," the detective went on.

So, slowly, and with the detective interrupting him on several occasions, picking him up on points, making him go back and clarify things, he told of the night when Baz had hit the old man. And all the time the detective remained expressionless so Lol could not tell whether he believed him or not.

When he had finally finished there was silence as the detective studied him.

"Right." The detective plonked his hands down on the table with a bang and stood up. He went and opened the door.

Lol, still seated, turned to look over his shoulders and felt a terrible wrenching in his chest when his parents walked in. He flung himself from the chair and threw himself into his father's arms. They stayed like that, locked together in a bear hug for quite a while before Lol broke away and hugged his mother too.

"There are just a few formalities to iron out, if you don't mind," the detective told them "I'd like your son to make a statement about the accident. As he is a juvenile, I would like you to remain present. As you were no doubt informed, Mr Jackson has been with him throughout the questioning."

"Yes, of course," Lol's father agreed. "Thank you, Mr Jackson, for all your help." He held out his hand to Jacko who firmly shook it.

"If you'll excuse me, I'll be off now," he told them. "I'll see you tomorrow," he said to Lol. "There's still a lot of work to be done on Bessie."

"Right," Lol agreed.

Laboriously, under the watchful eye of Sgt Henderson, Lol wrote down exactly what had happened. It filled two full sides of the big lined pages and afterwards, the detective read it aloud to him and he signed it. Only then did he finally believe it was the beginning of the end.

"What will happen now?" Lol's father asked the detective, after he had carefully placed the statement in a buff folder.

"We-ll." He was suitably non-commital. "I'm afraid it's not really up to me. Of course it is in Laurence's favour that he told the truth — and helped with the arrest of the other two. I'm afraid the decision will have to be made by someone much more important than me. I wouldn't worry *too* much about it. though."

Chapter Eight

Rocket rushed out of his basket and greeted them joyously when they finally arrived home. It was late and Lol found he was exhausted.

"Egg and chips?" his mother suggested.

"Fantastic. I'm famished."

"I expect you're half-starved," she said, making saucepans clatter as she began to get his meal ready.

"Gill did bring me some food — but that seems ages ago now."

He felt slightly self-conscious as he ate his meal hungrily, kcenly watched by his parents. Slowly, bit by bit, he filled them in on what had happened; the crash in Bessie, the row with the other boys and finally the car chase with Baz and Greg.

"I blame myself," his mother suddenly said tearfully.

Lol was amazed. What is she going on about? he thought.

"I should have guessed something was wrong. Why, even Mr Jackson mentioned the row with the other boys but I thought nothing of it."

"Mum," Lol protested. "Don't be silly. It was my fault. I was really stupid."

"You should have told us about crashing that banger of yours, if it was so important. We might have been able to help," his father told him.

"I thought you wouldn't want to hear anything more about the Project." Lol didn't intend to sound so bitter and when he saw the fleeting look of guilt cross his father's face he was instantly sorry.

"Perhaps there was some misunderstanding on all sides. We're all a bit to blame. Now I suggest we all get a good night's sleep. Leave the washing up, mother, we'll do it tomorrow."

When he went upstairs Lol dispensed with washing his face, that could come in the morning. It was bliss to sink down in a comfortable bed again and draw soft bedclothes over him rather than a smelly old tarpaulin.

Within minutes he was asleep. A deep untroubled sleep and he woke in the morning he felt drowsy but content. He was surprised when he looked at his watch and found it was nearly ten o'clock.

"I thought I'd let you sleep in this

morning," his mother explained when she appeared with a cup of tea and a plate of toast on a tray. "I'm sure they can spare you from school for one day.

"Mind you — don't think you're going to get this treatment every day. Tomorrow it's back to normal."

"Has Dad gone?"

"No, he's on lates. He's downstairs on the phone."

"The phone, who to?"

"Oh I don't know. He'll tell you, I dare say, when you get down."

It was more than forty minutes before Lol did eventually appear downstairs washed and dressed in clean clothes. His father was sitting beside the telephone, yellow pages in his hand, a pad of paper and pencil by his side. He was holding the receiver to his ear, obviously waiting for the person on the other end to answer.

"You did say that banger of yours was a Standard Vanguard?" he asked, cupping his hand over the mouthpiece.

"Yes, why?"

"Hold on, hello, is that Hobson's — good. Can you tell me if you have a Standard Vanguard? A Standard Vanguard. Thank you." He turned to Lol, again cupping his hand over the mouthpiece. "He's checking."

"Hello. Yes, I'm still here. You do, that's excellent, thank you very much. Yes, I understand. Thank you."

"What on earth are you doing?"

"You said the back axle on your banger was broken."

"Yes."

"Well I've just found a replacement."

"A replacement?" This was all proving too much for Lol. "Where?"

"Hobson's. It's right on the other side of town, but the axle's ours if we want it."

"That's fantastic, Dad. Let's go."

"There is one small probem."

Lol's heart sank. There would be, wouldn't there, he thought wryly.

"It's still on the wreck and he hasn't got anyone there who can dismantle it."

"Can't you do it?"

"I could help," his father agreed, "but I don't know if I could manage the whole job myself. And I don't have that much time. I've got to be at work by 2 pm."

Lol could see the dream of Bessie going in the contest fading fast again.

"I could ask Jacko." It was a brain-wave.

"Good idea. You give him a ring and I'll see if I can find some overalls that will fit me."

The phone rang and rang and at first Lol thought Jacko must be out but eventually, very out of breath from running, he picked it up.

"Jacko, it's me — Lol."

"Hello, Lol — not got yourself in any more trouble, have you?"

"Very funny. Listen, I've found a back axle, or rather Dad's found a back axle."

"A back axle?" For a moment Jacko was confused. "Oh, you mean for Bessie. That's wonderful. Where?"

"Hobson's."

"How much? Don't forget we have almost nothing in the kitty."

Lol had forgotten that. Cupping his hand over the mouthpiece he hissed to his father, "He says how much does it cost? We haven't got much money."

"Tell him he needn't worry about that. It will be my treat."

Lol stared at his father in amazement, and it was only the disembodied voice of Jacko shouting from the receiver that brought him back to reality.

"He says he'll pay for it," Lol found he was shouting the good news.

"A sort of thank you to the boys," his father added.

"He says a sort of thank you," Lol passed on the message.

"Yes, I heard," Jacko told him laughing. "That's very generous."

"The trouble is he doesn't reckon he can dismantle it on his own. Can you come and help?"

There was a brief silence as Jacko considered.

"I don't see why not. Give me about an hour. I'll see you there."

"O.K. See you. 'Bye." And Lol replaced the receiver.

Hobson's was a huge scrap yard with hundreds of carcasses of cars in various stages of cannibalization. When Lol's father had parked his car they both made their way into the woodshed that served as a yard office. A large Alsatian in the corner snarled threateningly at them.

"Don't worry about him," the man in the office told them. "He won't hurt you so long as I'm here. Now, which car was it you was interested in?"

"The Standard Vanguard."

"Ah yes, the Vanguard. Nice solid car that, not that anyone seems interested in that sort of car any more. It's all chrome and flashy lights, that's what they like now. Come on, I'll show it to you." As he went out of the shed the dog got up and softly padded behind, keeping a wary amber eye on Lol and his father.

"There you are." The man pointed to a car standing almost on its own at the end of the yard. Despite being battered it was in a surprisingly good state of repair.

"How many yards did you have to try before you found this one 'ere," the man asked, a crooked smile on his face.

"Only two — we were lucky. And another yard said they could get one for us."

Lol stared at his father. He had told him he'd had to ring seventeen yards before he found a Vanguard. But the smug expression had disappeared from the man's face.

"Now shall we talk about money before you begin?"

"Thirty pounds," Lol's father said

immediately. Lol blanched. That was a fortune.

"Do me a favour," the man said, pushing his cap on to the back of his head. "Eighty quid."

"Thirty-five — and that's providing it's not damaged in any way."

"Seventy-five."

"Forty."

"Seventy. And that's my last offer."

"Sorry to have troubled you," his father began, walking away. "We'll just have to leave it. We could get a whole new banger for seventy. Come on, Lol, we should just make it round to the other yard." Lol's face fell but he hurried to join his father.

" 'Old on, 'old on, don't be so 'asty," the man finally called after them and Lol's father winked at Lol.

"Forty it is — and it's daylight robbery."

"Have you got a jack we could use?"

"Over there," the man gestured towards a large garage jack lying by the shed. "And I suppose you want me to give you a hand dismantling it too."

"That would be very kind, but we do have a friend coming," Lol's father told him and the man strode off, the dog following close behind him.

"O.K., let's get started."

"Shouldn't we wait for Jacko?"

"We can get most of the donkey work done first and then he can do the fancy stuff."

By the time they heard footsteps approaching, the car was carefully raised on the jack.

"You're doing a good job," Jacko called to them.

Lol couldn't contain his delight when he turned round, for Jacko was not alone. Charlie Gibson was with him.

"Hello young Lol," Charlie said to him. "I hear you've been having a bit of an eventful time. Good afternoon, Mr. Lord, I'm Charlie Gibson."

"He's a champion stock car racer," Lol told his father admiringly.

"Was," Charlie corrected him. "Now I'm just a humble banger driver."

Lol's father directed the conversation back to the car.

"I think we've got it jacked up well enough."

"Looks like it," Charlie cast an expert eye over it. "I'll get the tools from the truck."

He returned with a huge blue metal box that when opened displayed six or seven large trays of tools.

Lol's father looked at his watch.

"If you don't mind, I'll just settle up with the chap in charge and then be off. Doesn't do to be late in to work."

"I hope you'll be along on Saturday to see the race," Jacko asked him as he got out of his overalls.

"I wouldn't miss it for the world."

It was hard, dirty work, dismantling

the axle. Once or twice Lol thought they would have to give up and return to the Project empty-handed but eventually, sweating and covered with tiny red flecks of rust, they managed to remove it intact and put it on the back of the truck.

When they returned to the Project they immediately got Bessie up on the ramps so they could begin work on her straight away.

By the time they had returned from a tea break inside Jacko's house the boys were beginning to arrive at the garage.

The jokes and the ever wilder stories about the previous day's adventures were already coming thick and fast.

"Man, did you see Lol's face when old Baz walked in," Biffo laughed.

"Yeah, but not nearly as good as old Baz when we bundled him into the van. I thought he was going to wet himself," Zac countered.

"And that punch he gave old Lol — *sock*," Alan gave a quick action replay, punching the air sharply.

"He could have broken my nose!" Lol felt he should mount some sort of defence. "Look, it's still swollen."

"Looks the same size as it always is," Biffo scoffed.

But a new sense of excitement swept through the garage when Jacko announced that they had got a new axle for Bessie.

"Do you mean we could be in the

competition?" Biffo's voice was unbelieving.

"*Could,* that's the important word," said Jacko. "I don't want to promise anything. We haven't got much time but she could be ready."

Each of the boys was allocated specific jobs to do and they worked well into the night. Although Lol wanted to thank Biffo properly, in all the madness and chaos the moment never presented itself. Several times he looked up and caught Biffo's eye long enough to swap wide grins, but for most of the time each concentrated on his task.

At nine Charlie announced he would have to go and Lol walked out with him to the truck.

"Thanks very much, Charlie," he said. "We'd never have been able to fix her without your help."

"She's not ready yet," he warned Lol. "So don't count your bangers before they can move."

"Will you come along on Saturday?"

"Of course. Where would you lot be without my expert tuition. I'll see you in the car park."

An hour later Jacko finally told the boys they would have to call it a day.

"I'm going to be in terrible trouble with your parents as it is," he said. "Do any of you want me to walk you home as it's so dark?"

He grinned as they jeered noisily at him.

"Can we come to work on her tomorrow night," John asked, voicing the request they had all intended to make.

"I suppose so," Jacko told them. "But my wife is going to kill me. I don't get overtime, you know."

Biffo and Lol walked up the lane together and it felt as if the events of the past ten days had just been a dream.

"He's pretty good, isn't he," Lol said.

"Who?"

"Jacko."

"Fantastic."

"Yes."

"Do you think we can get her finished on time?"

"Bessie?"

"Yes."

" 'Course we can, a super team like ours."

"Biffo?"

"Yes."

"Thanks for helping me out yesterday, I really appreciate it."

"Hey man. No problem. What are friends for?"

"Goodnight."

"See you tomorrow."

"Yeah, see you tomorrow."

The boys all worked harder than they had ever done before. They arrived as soon as they could in the evening and worked until Jacko eventually evicted them. But she was really taking shape.

Zac and David had worked on welding the doors shut and Gill had been allowed to give her a new coat of paint.

"How are we going to get her to the stadium?" John asked on Friday night while they waited for Biffo to return from putting her through her somewhat sedate paces down the track.

"Charlie's loaning us his truck and trailer."

"What time do we have to start out?"

"The race is scheduled for three o'clock so I reckon we should get there for midday. That will give us plenty of time to make last-minute adjustments."

"Do you want us to give you a hand loading her up?"

"Is that an unsubtle hint that you all want to come to the stadium in the van?" Jacko countered.

"Will there be room for us all?"

"We'll make room."

The next morning Lol was awake early. His overalls, freshly washed, were on the chair and he pulled them on straight away over his jeans and jersey. Finally he pulled his cycling cap down low over his forehead then surveyed himself in the mirror.

"Pretty impressive" he told himself out loud. "A touch of the James Hunts."

"You *do* look the part," his mother commented as she eyed him appreciatively.

"Smooth, eh?" he preened himself and she laughed at him.

"Sit down and eat your breakfast. I've made you some lunch," and she patted a bulging plastic carrier bag.

"For everyone?" There seemed enough to feed an army.

"That's enough of your cheek. I don't want you eating any of those disgusting hot dogs — heaven knows what's in them."

"Alsatian?"

"Quite probably. Anyway I've done some cheese, and some beef, and some egg and cress ones. And there are some apples. Do you want tea or coffee?"

"I've got some milk." He indicated the full beaker in front of him.

"No, silly, in the thermos."

"Mu-um," he protested. "I can't take a flask!"

"You'll be very glad of it later, you wait and see. I'll give you coffee."

"All right." He bolted down the last of his breakfast. He knew he would never win once his mother had made up her mind. "Where's Dad?"

"Gone down to do the shopping. He doesn't want to be stuck in Sainsbury's when he should be cheering you on."

"Are you coming?" He couldn't imagine banger racing being exactly his mother's cup of tea.

"Of course. I've asked Auntie Edie to video it."

"They'll probably put football on instead," he muttered, unable to believe that this longed-for afternoon would go off without a hitch.

"Rubbish. Off you go, and we'll see you later."

Despite his early start he was almost the last one to arrive and there was feverish activity in the garage.

"Radiator — the cap's on its way out," John told him. "There's a spare one somewhere but we just can't find it."

"Ask Gill, she knows where everything is."

The new radiator cap was found and fitted then it was the rear tyre that caused sudden concern.

"For heaven's sake, does it matter if it has got a slow puncture," Biffo shouted. "Just so long as it stays up long enough to get her on the track?"

By noon, with still no sign of Charlie's truck, tempers were beginning to become a little frayed.

"Wouldn't you know. We go mad to get her ready and now we can't get her to the race track." Even Tom, who rarely strung two words together, was beginning to get agitated.

"It's here!"

As the van and trailer turned into the drive there was a scramble to open the garage doors and reverse Bessie out.

"All together, push," Charlie instructed

from the driver's seat as he guided her up on to the trailer.

Quickly they roped her to the trailer then with a last glance back at the garage to check they had not forgotten anything, they began to climb into the van.

Lol lost the battle to get in the front but later he was glad. It was a terrific atmosphere all crammed in the back of the van, the smell of oil filling their nostrils, the excitement making them keep up a non-stop barrage of chatter.

After a brief word with the steward on the gate, Charlie swung the van and trailer expertly into the allotted space. Already several other teams were beginning to unload their bangers and the boys eyed them intently.

"This section is for all those competing in the youth section," Charlie told them. "They've put the others in the north car park. Right, we'll begin to get Bessie off and then we'll register. Who's driving?"

There was absolute silence. Surprised, he glanced across the row of faces.

"Well you'd better make a decision soon. They'll want to register the driver."

When Jacko arrived about ten minutes later with Gill that was the first question he faced.

"I hadn't forgotten," he told them. "In fact I've been giving it a lot of thought. Any of you got any suggestions?"

"I suppose Lol should really, his Dad paid for the new axle," John said, and a few of the others nodded.

Lol was intensely embarrassed. He knew that although no one said it they were all thinking that he had also broken the first one.

"Let's draw lots," he said. "You said we're all good drivers, then let's just draw lots."

"Does that sound fair to you all?" Jacko asked and it was agreed.

Gill produced a piece of paper out of her pocket and someone else found a stub of pencil.

"Right," she said, obviously enjoying her moment in charge. "I'll tear up the paper into ten pieces and put a cross on one. Then we'll put them in a hat and everyone draws one out. The person with the cross gets to drive."

They all nodded agreement and watched as she tore the paper into rough pieces then put a large pencil cross on one piece.

"Who's got a hat?"

Alan pulled Lol's off his head and held it out. Gill carefully scooped up the paper pieces and put them in the hat, giving it a little wiggle to mix them up.

"Who's first?"

There was silence as they looked at each other.

"Oh, let me, I can't stand the suspense!" Zippo held out his hand and, eyes shut, took one of the pieces of paper.

"Nothing," he said miserably when he

had opened it. The others breathed a sigh of relief.

Gradually they all took one and opened them, shaking their heads with disappointment as the elusive cross evaded them. Finally there was only Biffo, Alan and Lol with the paper still in their hands, unopened.

Carefully, Alan opened his. "Not me," he declared.

Biffo and Lol stared at each other then, almost fold for fold, they opened their pieces of paper.

"Congratulations," Lol said, holding out his hand to Biffo, whose face split in a huge grin.

"Let me at them," Biffo said, moving his hands wildly, as if wrapped around an invisible steering wheel. "I'll hammer them, I'll bash them. They won't stand a chance."

"Yeah well, before you do all that I suggest we go and register you. The rest of you check that Bessie is worthy of such an illustrious driver."

Lol felt a pang of jealousy as he watched Biffo and Jacko walk off towards the stadium.

"Do you mind very much?" Gill handed him back his hat.

" 'Course not. Biffo's a really good driver."

"As good as you?" she teased.

"Maybe not quite *that* good, but adequate, adequate."

Soon the air resounded to the angry roaring of engines and you took your life in your hands to cross the cinder car park. Everywhere youngsters, some so small they didn't seem able to look over the steering wheel, took the opportunity to practise.

Several times the tannoy called out, reminding them that the speed limit in the car park was five miles an hour, but it seemed to have no effect.

Biffo, helmet jammed down over his head, had three practice runs.

"How does it feel?" Charlie asked him when he returned from the first one.

"Not bad. It pulls a bit to the right."

"Look, if that's all that's wrong with it don't complain, not unless it starts pulling you round in circles."

Lol, Jacko and Alan decided that while Biffo was brushing up on his driving technique they would take a look at the opposition.

They counted twelve cars in all, but four Jacko discounted almost immediately.

"Engines sound too rough," he explained. "They'll never last the course — and that one," he pointed to a yellow-and-white Anglia, "will never get going at all."

Eventually they narrowed the main rivals down to four cars. Two from London, one from Birmingham, and one from a public school in Wales. They had just finished passing all this on to Biffo when the first announcement for the junior championship went out over the tannoy.

Races had been going on for some time in the stadium and every so often a loud cheer would fill the air.

"How'd you feel?" Lol asked Biffo, as he helped him fasten the safety harness round his wiry body.

"Magic, man, pure magic."

"Good luck."

And Biffo gave a double thumbs up before easing Bessie into gear and moving towards the opening into the stadium. The boys ran to join the other members of the teams in the entrants pits and waited for the announcer to call for the drivers. Lol scanned the packed stadium but realized it would be a miracle if he could see his parents. It was stupid, he should have arranged to meet them.

At last the announcement came and like giant metal gladiators the cars moved slowly into the ring, lining up two abreast on the perimeter track. Biffo was in the second row in the same position Charlie had been in in his race. Lol hoped it was a good omen.

As Jacko had predicted, the Anglia did not make it into the stadium so there were eleven cars prepared to do battle.

The stand-by hooter sounded and the scream of engines soared even louder. Then, as the hooter sounded again, there was a roar from the crowd — and the race began.

It was difficult to see clearly what was happening from the pits, so the boys took it in turns to climb on to the retaining wall for a better view.

"He's fourth," Zac commented to the others, "*Oooh.*"

"What's happened, what's happened?" they all demanded.

"It's all right, I thought he'd lost it on that bend but he managed to pull her back. That lead car is real good, I can't see him catching her."

"Of course he will." Lol pulled himself up beside Zac, the dust-filled air making his eyes smart.

After four circuits Biffo was in second place, strongly challenging the large blue car that had begun, and remained, in the lead position.

"Get him, Biffo, get him," Joseph shouted, then let out a piercing yelp of glee as, just going into the final bend, Bessie hit the blue car squarely on the back wing and sent it spinning off, leaving a gap just large enough for her to get through.

"He's going to do it, he's going to do it," they all yelled as the two cars raced, almost neck and neck, down the final straight.

Ridiculously none of them actually saw the final moments of the race. Standing clinging together all trying to watch the excitement, the presence of eight boys proved too much for the small space available, and with a loud cry of anguish they fell together in a crumpled heap on the concrete floor.

When they finally managed to pick themselves up they saw Jacko hurrying towards them.

"Not bad was it?" he said, obviously delighted.

"Did we win?" The same cry went up from each boy.

"We were second," he said, confused. "Weren't you watching?"

He got no explanation. They all fell on each other, the momentary disappointment that they had not pulled off the dream victory replaced by wild euphoria.

"Second's fantastic! Second — can you believe that."

They raced round to the car park just in time to see Biffo coming out of the stadium entrance.

As he pulled himself out of the window, helmet still in place, they picked him up and carried him shoulder-high in a wide sweep of the car park.

Afterwards, when they had finished loading Bessie back onto the trailer, Jacko called them together and produced a large bottle of lemonade and a pack of paper cups.

"I'm sorry it can't be something stronger," he said, pouring a little into each cup. "But I don't want to be carted off for serving alcohol to people under age.

"First, I think we should toast Biffo who did brilliantly well to come second — and winning £50 in the process." They all cheered and Biffo gave several little bows to the group.

"Second, we should toast the finest mechanics in the country — that's you lot, in case you didn't recognize yourselves." Another cheer went up.

"And finally." He paused, turning to look at Bessie, slightly battered now, on the trailer. "To Bessie."

"To Bessie," they all shouted, and this time the cheering was loudest of all.

Some Other Hippo Books to look out for:

THE THREE DETECTIVES AND THE MISSING SUPERSTAR

Simon Brett

0 590 70530 X £1.25

It was quite by chance that Emma Cobbett saw Dazzleman, lead singer of the chart-topping group Reddimix, leave the studio where her father was directing the group's new promotional video. She didn't really want the autograph the singer gave her before being driven away, but when it seems clear that Dazzleman has disappeared, everyone else thinks it is an exasperatingly mistimed publicity stunt. Emma has her doubts, especially when she discovers that she didn't get an autograph from Dazzleman at all, but a coded message!

With her friends Stewi and Marcus, Emma investigates the kidnapping of Dazzleman – a crime that only the Three Detectives believe has happened. As their enquiries continue – helped by the irrepressible Kimberley, Dazzleman's most devoted fan – the Three Detectives realise that the key to what they're dealing with lies in Dazzleman's mysterious past – and it's much more serious than it had seemed at first.

AM I GOING WITH YOU?

Thurley Fowler

0 590 70539 3 £1.25

' "Sydney, that's great."

"Not you dear. You can't go. This is my big chance to get into television. I'm sorry, Carlton, you just have to go to your Uncle Harry." '

Poor Carlton. Not only had he the burden of being named after a football team, but his mother was sending him away to his uncle while she went to Sydney. Carlton hated the farm and his cousin Simon. What if something happened to him at school? Who did you tell when your mother wasn't there?

Everything was different on the farm. From the moment he arrived he was in trouble. His uncle seemed to dislike him, his cousin tormented him. But life wasn't all black. On the cricket pitch he really came into his own. And eventually other things began to fall into place.

CRY VAMPIRE!

Terrance Dicks

0 590 70405 2   £1.25

Anna Markos had disappeared. The police had started a big hunt – but Simon and Sally knew they wouldn't find the young girl. They knew exactly where she was. But what could they do? Who on earth would believe them if they said she'd fallen into the clutches of vampires . . .?

Other Vampire stories for you to get your teeth into:

THE LITTLE VAMPIRE

Angela Sommer-Bodenburg

0 590 70132 0   £1.25

Tony loves stories about vampires but when the real thing lands on his window-sill one evening and introduces himself as Rudolph, he is not so enthusiastic!

THE LITTLE VAMPIRE MOVES IN

Angela Sommer-Bodenburg

0 590 70298 X   £1.00

When Rudolph, the little vampire, is banished from his home, Tony, his friend, lets him move into the basement – coffin and all! But soon, Tony is at his wits end trying to prevent his parents from finding out about the new tenant downstairs!

THE LITTLE VAMPIRE TAKES A TRIP

Angela Sommer-Bodenburg

0 590 70408 7 £1.25

The idea of a family holiday in boring Nether Bogsbottom becomes more interesting to Tony when the Little Vampire agrees to come along. But how will they get the coffin there in secret . . .?

THE LITTLE VAMPIRE ON THE FARM

Angela Sommer-Bodenburg

0 590 70443 5 £1.25 approx (to be published in September 1986)

Tony's problems were over – he had safely sneaked the little vampire into the holiday home at Nether Bogsbottom! But vampires live in coffins – and where do you hide one of those on a farm?

LAST SEEN ON HOPPER'S LANE

Janet Allais Stegeman

0 590 70435 4 £1.50

Kerry discovered the old, stone house on Hopper's Lane by chance and getting inside was not as hard as she thought it might be. Inside the air was cold and dead, like a tomb — the only sound was Kerry's own quick breathing.

Along the hallway was a drawing-room of such proportions that Kerry felt dwarfed, and in her mind's eye she imagined herself dressed in a dazzling gown, dancing to an orchestra. But as she waltzed and turned, Kerry's song choked to a terrified stop in her throat. There stood the ugliest little man she had ever seen, and he was pointing a gun at her.

"Don't move," he said. "And don't make a sound. Leave your hands up."

Kerry's whole body went rigid, her stomach heaved with fear.

"All right — walk in front of me!" And he jammed the point of the pistol in her back. "We're going to get in the van."

The back of the van was dim. Kerry was confused and frightened. But there was one thing of which Kerry was sure — she needed to get out of the van before it was too late . . . Kerry didn't want to be LAST SEEN ON HOPPER'S LANE!

And for Older Readers:

I WILL CALL IT GEORGIE'S BLUES

Suzanne Newton

0 590 70352 8 £1.95

Preacher's kids aren't any different to anyone else," I said stiffly.

"Maybe not, but they should be."

To the residents of Gideon, North Carolina, Neal, Aileen and Georgie Sloan constitute the "perfect" minister's family. But life for the children of Richard Sloan is tougher than it looks, and the happy public face hides and strains and secrets that are forcing the family apart.

Neal finds himself in an impossible position; trying to please his relentlessly strict father, struggling to remain friends with his rebellious older sister - who is in danger of failing to graduate from High School to the shame of the family - and trying to win the trust of and reassure his little brother Georgie, who suffers from his own dark and engulfing fears. Neal is forced to keep his own passion for playing jazz piano a close secret between himself and their neighbour, Mrs Talbot, for without this release he fears for his own stability. But Georgie is the catalyst. Seams begin to unravel in the perfect family fabric until catastrophe forces Georgie over the edge of sanity.